SOMETHING'S ROTTEN
IN THE TOWN OF CHEYENNE . . .

LUKE TRAVIS: The lawman who's cleaning up Abilene goes to Cheyenne to find out who framed Ruth Carson—before it's too late!

CODY FISHER: The headstrong young deputy is on his own while the marshal's out of town. And he's determined to keep Abilene in line . . .

RUTH CARSON: The feisty newspaperwoman has her share of enemies—and now they've got her by the neck! It's an open-and-shut case of murder—until Travis rides into town . . .

P. K. NELSON: He looks more like a salesman than a traveling merchant of death. For once, the affable hangman is stumped. Is it possible that "he who never hanged an innocent man" is about to put an innocent woman to death?

FLINT McCABE: Now that his partner Mayor Yates is dead, nothing stands between McCabe and marriage to Yates's beautiful daughter, consolidating their vast spreads. Nothing can stop him—until Luke Travis noses in where he doesn't belong . . .

JOEL WRAY: He's in love with the woman his boss, Flint McCabe, wants to marry. But can he save her from a fate she doesn't desire . . . ?

Most Pocket Books are available at special quantity discounts for bulk purchases for sales promotions, premiums or fund raising. Special books or book excerpts can also be created to fit specific needs.

For details write the office of the Vice President of Special Markets, Pocket Books, 1230 Avenue of the Americas, New York, New York 10020.

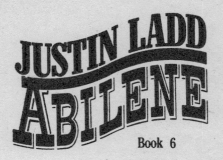

JUSTIN LADD
ABILENE

Book 6

THE HANGMAN

Created by the producers of
**Wagons West, Stagecoach,
White Indian, and San Francisco.**

Book Creations Inc., Canaan. NY · Lyle Kenyon Engel. Founder

POCKET BOOKS

New York **London** **Toronto** **Sydney** **Tokyo**

An *Original* Publication of POCKET BOOKS

Copyright © 1989 by Book Creations, Inc.
Cover art copyright © 1989 Gordon Crabb

ISBN: 0-671-66991-5

First Pocket Books printing February 1989

10 9 8 7 6 5 4 3 2 1

POCKET and colophon are trademarks of Simon & Schuster Inc.

Printed in the U.S.A.

Prologue

JUDGING BY THE HIGHLY CHARGED ATMOSPHERE IN THE packed courtroom in Cheyenne, Wyoming Territory, there was nothing more exciting than a murder trial—except maybe a hanging. And it looked as if the inhabitants of this rugged frontier town would be seeing *that* in the near future.

As the members of the jury filed into the courtroom on this bright July afternoon and took their seats in the jury box they looked grim. They were simple, solid citizens—storekeepers, farmers, bartenders—and the responsibility of deciding someone else's fate weighed heavily upon them. But they had been given a life-or-death decision to make, and evidently, they had made it.

Once the jury was seated, the bailiff went to the door to the left of the judge's bench and knocked lightly on it. A moment later the door opened, and Judge Franklin Shaw appeared framed in the doorway, shrugging his black robe onto his broad shoulders. Everyone stood as the tall, imposing man entered the courtroom and stepped behind the bench. He squinted at the jury from under bushy eyebrows and grimaced. He did not like what he saw in their faces, but he was not surprised.

Judge Shaw sat down, and the others in the room followed suit. He glanced at the defense table and saw the tense, anxious expression on the defendant's face. She was an attractive, middle-aged brunette who looked as if she should be baking bread or clerking in a milliner's shop—almost anything other than standing on trial for her life. Next to her sat her lawyer, a fussy little man with a mustache, who appeared even more worried than his client.

The judge rapped his gavel on the bench and grunted, "This court is back in session." Turning to the jury foreman, he asked, "Has the jury reached a verdict in this matter?"

As the bespectacled, round man stood up, he mopped beads of sweat from his face. He nodded and said, "We have, Your Honor."

Judge Shaw told the defendant, "Miss Carson, you will rise and face the jury."

Ruth Carson hesitated and glanced nervously at her attorney. Beside her, Kenneth Blanchard reached out and put a hand on her arm, squeezing lightly. Ruth nodded, then stood, her features now composed. She was obviously making a great effort to appear calm, but she was a strong woman.

"What is your verdict, gentlemen?" Judge Shaw asked.

The jury foreman solemnly intoned, "We find the defendant guilty as charged."

As soon as the words were out of his mouth, the taut silence in the packed courtroom ended abruptly. Excited muttering erupted among the crowd. Many of the spectators seemed upset by the verdict, but the pleased grins on the faces of others indicated that they agreed with the jury.

Ruth Carson showed little emotion as the verdict was read. Her hands started to clench into fists, then suddenly relaxed. Although her shoulders did not slump, for a moment an air of resignation passed over her.

She remained standing as Judge Shaw looked back at her. He took a deep breath and asked, "Do you have anything to say in your behalf before I pass sentence on you, Miss Carson?"

Ruth shook her head. "I've already told my story, Your Honor," she said. "There's nothing more to say."

"In that case . . . Ruth Carson, you have been found guilty in the murder of Mayor Roland T. Yates. Therefore, in accordance with the laws of the Territory of Wyoming, I proclaim that you will be hanged by the neck until dead, said execution to take place at nine o'clock, Friday morning, one week from today." The judge's voice shook slightly as he passed sentence. He had been devoted to the law for decades, and the law was clear in this case. Still, this was the first time he had ever sentenced a woman to death. He banged his gavel again and growled over the hubbub in the courtroom, "This court is adjourned. Bailiff, turn the defendant over to the sheriff's men."

Ruth Carson accepted the sentence as stoically as

she had the verdict. Now she turned to her lawyer and said, "I'm sorry, Kenneth."

Blanchard stood up and put his hands on her shoulders. "I'm the one who's sorry, Ruth," he said fervently. "I did everything I knew. . . ."

She patted one of his hands and smiled slightly. "I know. Don't worry, Kenneth."

The bailiff came up beside her and said, "Let's go, Miss Carson."

"Just one moment, please?" Ruth asked. Turning back to Blanchard, she went on quickly, "There is one more thing you can do for me, Kenneth."

"Anything, Ruth, you know that."

"I want you to send a telegram. There's one man who might still be able to help me." A small flame of hope flickered in her eyes. "If anyone can prove my innocence in time to save me, it's Marshal Luke Travis of Abilene, Kansas."

Chapter One

MARSHAL LUKE TRAVIS DUCKED AS A BULLET FLEW over his head. He was crouched behind a water trough on Abilene's Texas Street. Lying on his belly a couple of feet away was Deputy Cody Fisher.

Cody glanced at Travis and said, "One of us is going to have to shoot him, Marshal."

From across the street came a crazed howl. Travis lifted his head long enough to take a quick look. He saw a tall, burly man in a buffalo coat staggering on the boardwalk in front of the Bull's Head Saloon. There was an old Walker Colt in the man's right hand, and tucked under the same arm was a Sharps Big Fifty buffalo gun. In his left hand the man held a bottle of whiskey, which he lifted to his mouth for a long swig as Travis watched. When he finally lowered the bottle, he howled again and then loosed another shot from the revolver, this one smacking into the wall of the apothecary nearby.

"He's just drunk, Cody," Travis muttered. "You know old Nestor as well as I do. He doesn't mean to hurt anybody."

"Maybe not, but he's going to if he keeps shooting like that. He *would* go on a binge on Saturday afternoon when everybody's in town."

Travis nodded grimly. He knew his deputy was right. Nestor Gilworth had been a buffalo hunter for years, until the once vast herds had shrunk almost to nothing, the scant remainder migrating south out of Kansas. Now Nestor did odd jobs to get along and caused little trouble—except when he went on one of his periodic drinking sprees. This was the worst one yet. As Cody said, somebody was going to get killed.

Travis raised his voice. "Nestor, you'd better put that gun down!" he called. "Stop shooting and nobody will get hurt!"

Nestor's reply was a hoot of drunken laughter and another round from the Colt.

Travis glanced up and down the street. The boardwalks along Texas Street were empty. Everyone who had been on them had scattered when Nestor flung the bartender through the saloon's window and then leapt after him with a gun in his hand. The dazed bartender had scrambled back into the saloon through the batwings while the townspeople scurried for cover.

The commotion had drawn Travis and Cody from the marshal's office, but they had to dive out of the line of fire themselves as Nestor shot at them. The old buffalo hunter was so drunk he was firing at anything that moved.

Travis slipped the long-barreled Colt from the holster on his hip. He knew he could stand up and put a bullet in Nestor before the drunken man could even start to fire. But Luke Travis had taken the job as marshal of Abilene—going against his own vow never to pin on a star again—in order to prevent as much bloodshed as possible in his adopted town. He would not kill Nestor Gilworth unless he had to.

Travis slid his gun back in its holster and said to Cody, "Distract him. Put a few bullets into the boardwalk at his feet."

"Why don't I just shoot him in the leg?" Cody asked.

Travis shook his head. "That wouldn't stop Nestor. It would just make him madder, and he'd still be able to shoot."

"What are you going to do?"

"Just get his attention," Travis snapped. Before Cody could argue, he rolled out from behind the water trough and surged to his feet.

Cody grimaced and raised himself to fire. The Colt in his hand began cracking. Across the street Nestor started to turn toward Travis, his attention drawn by the marshal's sudden move, but the slugs slamming into the planks at his feet made him dance back awkwardly.

Travis dashed across the street. He leapt onto the boardwalk as Cody's gun went silent. Nestor turned toward him again, moving surprisingly quickly for a bulky man who had been guzzling whiskey for hours. But the marshal was quicker. He snatched his gun from its holster and lashed out with it. The long barrel cracked against the buffalo hunter's skull.

Nestor's filthy felt hat and his mane of shaggy hair cushioned the blow, but it was powerful enough to stagger him. Travis struck again. This time the barrel of his Colt hit Nestor's wrist, causing the big man to drop his gun. The Sharps slipped from under his arm and clattered to the boardwalk.

Roaring like a wounded bear, Nestor lunged. His long arms reached out and encircled Travis. The marshal found himself pressed against his opponent with his arms pinned to his sides. The stench from the buffalo coat that the man wore year-round almost overwhelmed him, but as Nestor's arms tightened in a vicious hug, Travis discovered that he could not breathe anyway.

He brought his knee up, slamming it into Nestor's groin. The man grunted in pain and relaxed his grip on Travis just enough for the marshal to work his right arm free. Travis swung his Colt again. The barrel thudded twice against Nestor's head before his eyes rolled up and his muscles sagged. The marshal tore himself out of Nestor's grip and staggered back, panting for breath, as the buffalo hunter wobbled and then collapsed heavily on the boardwalk. Travis felt the planks quiver beneath his boots.

Glancing up, he saw Cody standing nearby, gun in hand in case more bullets were needed. Travis drew a full, deep breath and then gasped, "I told you we wouldn't have to kill him."

Cody grinned. "No, but I was starting to think you were going to have to hit him for an hour before he realized he ought to fall down."

Now that the commotion on the street had subsided, Abilene's citizens began poking their heads out of doorways to see if it was safe to emerge. The marshal holstered his gun and waved to several men. "Throw some ropes on him and drag him if you have to," Travis told them, pointing to Nestor's sprawled bulk, "but get him to the jail and put him in one of the cells. I don't think he'll be waking up anytime soon. He's got a lot to sleep off."

"Sure, Marshal," one of the men replied. His companions and he began trying to lift Nestor and haul him to jail.

Travis and Cody stood on the boardwalk and watched the operation. The two lawmen made a formidable pair. Even as winded as he was, Luke Travis was an impressive man. Tall, with narrow hips and broad, powerful shoulders, he had worked hard for all of his forty-odd years. Most of his time was spent in town these days, so he wore a dark suit and a string tie. The badge pinned to his vest glinted in the sunlight. He was no townie, though, as his boots, broad-brimmed black hat, and well-cared-for gun belt testified. He had thick brown hair and a full mustache that drooped slightly over his wide mouth.

Cody Fisher was a lot younger and a lot more casual in his dress. He could have been taken for a drifting cowhand had it not been for the gun on his hip. The holster was low-slung and the Colt's pearl grips were worn smooth from use. It was a gunfighter's rig, and that was exactly what Cody might have been if he had not met Luke Travis and wound up on the side of the law. The deputy's quick grin flashed as he watched the townsmen struggling with Nestor Gilworth's huge body.

"Sort of like trying to throw a buffalo in the hoosegow, isn't it?" Cody asked. "You figure Nestor got to looking like that because he spent so much time with those ugly critters?"

"Could be," Travis grunted.

"What are you going to do with him?"

"Keep him locked up until he's sober," Travis replied. "He'll have to serve some time for disturbing the peace, too. Then I think I'll try to talk him into moving on. Folks around here are getting tired of his ruckuses. Somebody's liable to shoot him next time."

"Seems like they'd have good cause."

Travis could not argue with that. "Like I told those boys, I don't expect Nestor to wake up anytime soon, but you'd better go over there and keep an eye on things, just in case he comes to before they lock him up. I could use a drink, so I think I'll walk down to Orion's."

Cody nodded and started across the street toward the jail.

Travis began walking west down Texas Street toward the tavern where his good friend Orion McCarthy served the best whiskey, the coldest beer, and the tallest tales in Abilene. The marshal had taken only a few steps when he heard someone calling his name. He turned and saw one of the clerks from the Western Union telegraph office hurrying toward him.

"Telegram for you, Marshal," the man said breathlessly as he reached Travis. "I think it's pretty important."

Travis nodded. "Thanks, Max," he said, and took the yellow telegraph form from the clerk. As he scanned the words printed there, his lean features tightened into a bleak, angry expression.

"Max, this was sent yesterday. See here, it's dated Friday." He pointed to the form and peered at the clerk.

"Marshal, I'm sorry," Max began, "but the lines

between Cheyenne and Denver were down all last night. We don't know what happened. This just came in. Any reply, Marshal?" he asked somewhat nervously.

Travis nodded. "Wire Cheyenne," he said hoarsely. "Tell the lady I'll be there as soon as I can." Then he turned and strode toward his office, the drink he had been anticipating completely forgotten.

When the marshal reached the jail, he found that the townsmen had managed to haul Nestor into one of the cells. The men were standing around puffing and panting as Cody swung the cell door shut with a clang. They all looked around as Travis entered the office and went to his desk.

Cody saw the expression on Travis's face and knew something was wrong. "Thanks, boys," he said to the others. "We'll take care of Nestor now."

"Behind bars is the best place for him," one of the men muttered. "He ain't nothin' but an animal."

The townsmen trooped out of the office. Travis did not look up as they left. His eyes were fastened on the telegram he had dropped on the desk in front of him.

Cody shut the cellblock door and strolled to the side of the desk, eyeing the yellow paper. Whatever was on that paper had upset Travis. "What's wrong, Marshal?" he asked.

Travis grunted and shoved the telegram toward his deputy. "Read that," he said.

Cody picked it up and quickly read the message.

CHEYENNE WYOMING TERRITORY JULY 5, 1878
NEED HELP WILL BE HUNG ONE WEEK FROM TODAY
FOR MURDER PLEASE COME RUTH CARSON

Cody looked up from the telegram and stared at Travis. "Sounds like bad business," he murmured. "Womenfolk don't usually hang, even for murder. This lady a friend of yours?"

The marshal shook his head. "My sister-in-law, Ruth Carson. I haven't seen her in years, not since Sarah was . . . hurt."

Travis did not need to mention that while he was marshal of Wichita his wife Sarah had taken a bullet meant for him, a bullet that did not kill her immediately but instead led to a slow, lingering death despite all that Travis and the best doctors in the East could do. Cody knew about that, knew that this telegram had stirred up those painful memories, in addition to the shocking news it contained.

The marshal took a deep breath. "The last I knew, Ruth was planning to move to Wyoming Territory to start a newspaper in Cheyenne. Publishing a paper, that was what she'd always dreamed of doing, and she figured Wyoming would be a good place for a woman to give it a try."

"I'd heard that they were letting women vote now in Wyoming." Cody nodded. "Seems like a mighty strange idea to me, but I guess that's their right. What do you think about this murder business?"

Travis shook his head. "It's unbelievable to me. Ruth doesn't have a violent bone in her body." He smiled humorlessly. "She and I didn't get along too well to start with. She didn't think too much of the line of work I was in, and then it just got worse after Sarah—" He broke off with another shake of his head. Then he put his hands on the desk and pushed himself to his feet. "I've got to go see what this is all about."

"Sure. You want some company?"

Travis hesitated. "Thanks, Cody," he said after a moment. "I appreciate the offer. But somebody's got to stay here in Abilene to keep the peace. It looks to me like you're elected."

Cody nodded slowly. Being left in charge of a bustling, growing town like Abilene was a lot of responsibility, but the young deputy had taken on big jobs before. Both he and Travis knew he would be up to it.

Now that he had decided on his course of action, Travis began to issue orders crisply. "You'd better have Aileen take a look at Nestor, just to make sure I didn't hit him too hard. I don't think you could crack that skull of his with anything less than a sledgehammer, but there's no point in taking chances. Tell the prosecutor to charge Nestor with disturbing the peace. You can swear in Orion as a temporary deputy to give you a hand if you need it. I won't be gone much more than a week."

Neither Travis nor Cody needed to mention the significance of that period of time.

He slipped his watch out of his vest pocket and flipped it open, then nodded grimly. "There's a west-bound train due through here in about an hour. That'll be more than enough time to pack. I can take it to Denver and change trains for Cheyenne. Ought to be there day after tomorrow."

He hated to waste even that much time when he had only a week to save his sister-in-law's life. But there was no quicker way to get to Cheyenne. He would just have to work fast when he arrived.

Travis found it impossible to believe that Ruth had

killed anyone—unless it was an accident. Travis knew that in his bones. And even then, that was no call for a hanging. He vowed he would get to the bottom of this.

With a determined look on his lean face he strode out of the office, heading for his rented room to pack a bag.

Chapter Two

LUKE TRAVIS HAD NOT EXPECTED ANYONE TO COME TO the Kansas Pacific station to see him off. When he strode through the doors of the depot after buying his ticket, he was surprised to see Dr. Aileen Bloom and Orion McCarthy standing on the platform next to Cody Fisher.

Aileen came forward to meet him. She laid a hand on his arm and said, "Cody told us what's happened, Luke. I'm sure you'll be able to straighten it out."

Travis nodded. "Thanks. I hope you're right."

"Ye'll get to th' bottom o' this mess, Lucas," Orion assured him.

Despite the grim journey he was about to embark upon, he could not help but smile as he looked at his friends. Aileen, a very attractive brunette in her late twenties, had been serving Abilene well as its doctor. Orion was a burly Scotsman with powerful shoulders, shaggy red hair, and a full red beard shot with gray. Both of them were staunch friends of his, and Travis was glad to have them here to see him off. He could feel his spirits lifting.

"Did you get a chance to take a look at Nestor Gilworth's head?" he asked Aileen.

"He's got a pretty good lump on it," she replied with a nod. "He may have a slight concussion as well. It's hard to tell with Nestor, he's so addled. But I think he'll be fine once he's sober."

"He was singing hymns when we left the jail," Cody said, grinning. "Of course, he was making up his own words as he went along."

From the blush that colored Aileen's cheeks, Travis guessed that Nestor's improvised lyrics had been pretty coarse. He said to his deputy, "Just keep an eye on him."

"I will," Cody promised.

"An' I'll help out any way I can," Orion added. "Dinna worry ye head about Abilene while ye be gone, Lucas. Th' town will still be here when ye get back."

"I know." Travis chuckled. "A man gets used to taking care of a place, though. . . ." The keening whistle of an approaching train floated through the warm air of the summer afternoon. Travis glanced down the track. "That'll be the westbound train."

The train chugged into the station a few minutes later. Travis stowed his bag in the baggage car, then shook hands with Cody and Orion. "Don't worry, Marshal," Cody told him solemnly. "We'll take good care of things. And if you need any help, just send a wire and I'll be there."

"Thanks." Travis nodded. "So long, Cody, Orion."

Aileen rose on her toes to plant a quick kiss on his cheek. "Take care of yourself, Luke," she said softly.

Travis smiled at her for a moment, then turned and climbed up the steps into one of the passenger cars. Pausing on the platform, he lifted a hand to wave to his friends. Then he went into the crowded car and searched for a seat.

The train was scheduled to stop in Abilene for only a few minutes. Travis had just sat down when the whistle shrieked again, and the train lurched forward. Taking off his broad-brimmed hat, he placed it on the vacant seat next to him. He peered through the window to watch the depot glide out of sight. The train clattered slowly through the downtown area, then reached the trestle that crossed Mud Creek. Abilene's first settlers had built their homes and businesses along the banks of the creek, and some of the old huts were still standing.

The town had come a long way since then. It had grown from a collection of shanties linked by a series of muddy, rutted trails to a wild, brawling cowtown to the growing city it was today. It was a good town, and Travis felt a twinge of regret as he left it. But he did not doubt that he was doing the right thing. He could not ignore the trouble in which Ruth had somehow found herself.

As the last buildings of the town slid by and the train moved into the open prairie, Travis reached up, removed the badge from his vest, and slipped it into his pocket. He was leaving his jurisdiction now, heading into a territory where he would be only a common citizen like everyone else. He might run into trouble once he got there, and for the first time in quite a while, he would not have the power and authority of the law behind him. That knowledge made him feel vaguely uncomfortable.

What would he do if he reached Wyoming Territory and found himself on the wrong side of the law? Travis was going to have to think long and hard about how he would handle it.

The marshal noticed that there were only a few empty seats on the crowded train. Prosperous businessmen in suits sat beside immigrant families in threadbare clothes. A few cowboys were sprinkled among the passengers, as well as a solitary Indian who was squatting on the floor just inside the forward door of the car. Smoke, ashes, and soot from the engine blew in through the open windows and blended with the smoke from countless pipes, cigars, and cigarettes to create a blue haze that hung in the air. The acrid smoke and the stuffiness, along with the constant clatter of the wheels on the rails, gave Travis a slight headache. He was accustomed to being in the fresh air, but he knew he would have to tolerate these conditions for the length of this journey. He had no choice.

The train stopped in Salina, and even that short pause grated on Travis's nerves. Ever since he had read Ruth's telegram, he had become more acutely aware of the passage of time. When the engine finally lurched on its way again, he was relieved.

The next stop was the town of Ellsworth. By the time the train pulled into the depot Travis found that his headache had made him drowsy. He leaned his head against the hard back of the seat and closed his eyes. He had seen Ellsworth before; there was nothing here to interest him.

A few moments later, he heard the seat beside him squeak and felt a heavy thump as someone sat down. Travis opened his eyes and lifted his head to see who had joined him. He was glad he had thought to move his hat onto his lap before he closed his eyes.

The heavyset man had wide shoulders and brawny arms, and it was clear that his bulk was mostly muscle and not fat. He was wearing a brown tweed suit that fitted him snugly. Despite the heat, his collar was stiff and his tie in place. He took off a black derby to reveal dark, thinning hair, then turned to Travis. A wide grin split his broad, florid face.

"Good afternoon, sir," he said heartily. He thrust out a hand with blunt, thick fingers. "The name's P. K. Nelson."

"Luke Travis," the marshal grunted as he shook the man's hand. Nelson had a good grip, but not a crushing one.

"Where are you bound, friend?" Nelson was still grinning broadly.

"Cheyenne," Travis answered shortly. From the looks of the man's clothes and his jovial manner, he guessed that Nelson was a salesman of some sort.

"How about that?" Nelson said excitedly. "Cheyenne is where I'm headed, too. Going on business, are you?"

"That's right." Travis groaned inwardly. He was a bit dismayed at the prospect of spending any time sitting beside Nelson. He was in no mood for a drummer's long-winded gab.

"Me, too." Nelson's bushy black eyebrows rose and fell as he spoke. "Say, have you heard the story about the farmer and the donkey and the widow lady?"

Travis sighed as Nelson launched into the story

without waiting for a reply. At least he had not asked what Travis's business was. But he had not offered any explanation of what his own line was, which surprised Travis. He had expected that Nelson would be trying to sell him something by now.

As the train pulled out of Ellsworth, Nelson was well into his second story, which was as bawdy as the first. He did not seem bothered that Travis did not laugh at his jokes, because he furnished plenty of booming laughter of his own. Travis almost wished he was back in Abilene, confronting a drunken, homicidal Nestor Gilworth.

Night fell shortly, and Travis was able to get a brief respite from Nelson's never-ending stream of chatter while the man consumed several sandwiches that he purchased from the vendor who came through the car. Travis ate a sandwich himself, not really tasting it. His mind was still on Ruth's dilemma.

The marshal watched the night sliding by outside the window and paid little attention to P. K. Nelson's incessant prattle. Finally, he became aware that Nelson had fallen silent. He glanced over at him.

Nelson was peering back with a sheepish expression on his face. He seemed to be waiting for an answer to some question. Travis told himself to be polite. "I'm sorry, Mr. Nelson," he said. "My attention seems to have wandered. I've got a lot on my mind right now."

"Of course, of course. An important man like you would certainly have a lot to think about."

Travis frowned slightly. Did Nelson know he was a lawman? "What do you mean, important?" he asked, more sharply than he intended.

"No offense, friend," Nelson replied, holding up his big hands palm out. "I can tell by looking you're an

important man, that's all, and important men usually
have a lot on their minds."

Travis smiled wryly. "I'm not that important," he
said.

Nelson waved a hand to dismiss that thought.
"What I was saying is that this will be my first trip to
Cheyenne. I was just wondering what it's like. Have
you ever been there, Mr. Travis?"

"No." The marshal shook his head. "But I've heard
a great deal about it. It's supposed to be a pretty wild
place at times, although I've heard that Jeff Carr and
Wild Bill tamed it quite a bit."

Travis grimaced as soon as the words were out of his
mouth. The casual way he had spoken of the two
well-known lawmen, Thomas Jefferson Carr and
James Butler Hickok, hinted at a personal acquain-
tance with them. In fact, he had met both men, but
Nelson did not need to know that.

The implications of the reference had been lost on
Nelson, however. He started spinning a yarn about a
Wyoming rancher and a sheepherder.

Finally out of self-defense as much as anything,
Travis began to respond to Nelson's jokes with stories
of his own. At least it kept the man quiet for a few
minutes. By the time the conductor came through the
car to turn down the lamps so that people could sleep,
Travis found himself chuckling at some of the things
Nelson had to say.

All during the evening, Travis had expected the man
to pull out a whiskey flask. He had encountered very
few drummers who were not heavy drinkers. Apparently Nelson was not a tippler, however, because no
flask was produced.

Travis slept fitfully. He had never been able to sleep

well on trains, and Nelson's stertorous breathing did not make it any easier. By the time the dawn began lighting the sky, Travis was wide awake and peering out the window again. The train had not yet left Kansas, but up ahead, still far in the distance, the rising sun was glinting on the summits of the Colorado mountains. According to the rail schedule Travis had checked before he left Abilene, the train would reach Denver in the early evening. He would change trains there and ride all night, to arrive in Cheyenne just after sunup the next day. Then he could try to find out why anyone would be crazy enough to want to hang Ruth Carson for murder.

The train stopped at a small station, where, according to the conductor, breakfast could be purchased inside the depot. Travis stood up and tried to stretch his kinked muscles as Nelson roused fitfully from his sleep with a series of snorts and coughs.

"Want some breakfast?" Travis asked. "We're scheduled to stop here for a little while."

Nelson straightened in his seat and looked out the window past Travis. "Where the devil are we?"

"I didn't catch the name of the place."

"The back side of nowhere, I'd wager," Nelson grumbled. Evidently he was not his cheerful self first thing in the morning. "I hope they've cooked up plenty of hotcakes," he went on. "I could eat a dozen."

Looking at the man's bulk, Travis did not doubt it. He followed Nelson out of the car. About half of the passengers had gotten off, a few to leave the train here, most to eat breakfast. The ones who stayed on board either could not afford to buy food, having spent most of their money on their fares, or else did not choose to sample the food for sale at the depot. Travis knew that the second group of travelers might be smart; the meals at these stations were usually not very good.

Inside the depot's waiting room, there were no tables, only the usual hard wooden benches. The passengers ate sitting on them, holding their plates in their hands. Travis and Nelson joined the line of people that led past a wheeled cart that had been brought in to serve the meal. Each of them received a cup of weak coffee and a plate filled with a pale gelatinous mass. A pair of greasy sausages sat on top of the mound.

Nelson looked up from the plate that was thrust into his hand by the man who was serving from the cart. "What the devil is this mess?" he asked harshly.

"Grits an' sausage," the man answered in a slow Southern drawl. "What else y'all expect t' eat f' breakfast?"

"What about a stack of hotcakes and some hash-brown potatoes and maybe a steak?"

"Sounds good, doan it? But I ain't got it. What I got is grits an' sausage, take it or leave it. Best plate o' grits you'll find heah in Winona."

Travis tried not to grin too broadly at the expression on Nelson's face. The stuff on his plate did not look very appetizing, but he was hungry after the long night's ride. He handed a coin to the man and went to one of the benches, leaving Nelson to fume. Sitting down, he watched as Nelson sighed, paid for his breakfast, and strode over to join him.

"And to think that I believed civilization had come to this frontier with the arrival of the majestic iron horse," he said dramatically. He shook his head and stared down at the grits and sausage, then sighed again and began eating.

The food was better than it looked—which was not saying a great deal—and Travis was able to eat all of his. Nelson also emptied his plate. The two men finished their coffee, then strolled onto the station platform. The other passengers were drifting toward the train. From the way the conductor stood beside one of the cars, occasionally glancing at his watch, Travis knew that they would be pulling out soon. As far as he was concerned, it would not be soon enough. He was ready to get started again on the long journey to Cheyenne.

"All aboooooarddd!" the conductor bawled a few moments later. Travis and Nelson took their seats. Despite his complaints, the meal seemed to have lifted Nelson's spirits. He began telling Travis about a meal he had once had in San Antonio that was interrupted by a gun battle between a group of Texas Rangers and a band of Mexican bandits. Travis chuckled at the man's lurid account of diving for cover behind a giant pot of refried beans.

Nelson was quite a talker, but Travis realized that he was beginning to like the man. If nothing else, Nelson's yarns kept his mind off the problem he was facing, at least part of the time.

Once he was wound up, Nelson did not slow down. He kept talking all day long as the train left Kansas and crossed into Colorado, climbing into the foothills of the Rockies. The terrain became much more rugged, and as the tracks climbed steep grades and spanned deep gorges, Travis felt a growing admiration for the people who had built this railroad. It had been quite an accomplishment for all of them, from the surveyors and engineers down to the Irish laborers who had laid the tracks and blasted holes through the mountains. Even if the Kansas Pacific had lost the race to connect with the Central Pacific and be the first to span the continent, the line had nothing to be ashamed of.

Despite Nelson's amiable yarn-spinning, Travis became more tense as the day went on. By late afternoon, when the train finally approached Denver, it was all the lawman could do to stay in his seat. He wanted to get up and move, even if it meant pacing up and down the aisle of the car. With all his experience as a lawman, he should be calmer, he told himself sternly.

The telegram from Ruth had brought back so many memories of Sarah, though. . . .

Travis remembered now the way she had laughed, the shining sparkle in her eyes, how her lithe body felt in his arms as he embraced her, the taste of her sweet lips. And he remembered the way her health deserted her, how the injury sapped her strength until she simply had no reserves with which to fight for her life. But all during the ordeal, she never blamed him, never once suggested that if he had been a farmer or a rancher or a storekeeper—instead of a marshal— then that horrible fate would not have befallen her.

She loved him, from start to finish. It was that simple. And he loved her in return.

She would want him to help her sister if it was humanly possible.

The train pulled into Denver on schedule. Travis did not want to risk missing that northbound train to Cheyenne. He leapt from the car as soon as the wheels stopped turning, leaving a puzzled-looking P. K. Nelson behind him. He hurried to retrieve his bag, then raced to the ticket window.

But when Travis presented his ticket to the clerk, the man glanced at it and shook his head. "Sorry," he said. "That train's been delayed. It won't be here for three hours."

Travis caught his breath, and his hand tightened on the handle of his bag. "Three hours?" he repeated grimly.

"That's right. Your ticket is all in order. You can wait in the station if you like or go out to get something to eat. Just be back when the train gets in. It won't be here long; the crew will be trying to make up some of the lost time."

Travis swallowed the angry words that began to rise in his throat. It would not help to argue with the clerk. The man had no control over the trains. If one of them was late, no one could do anything about it.

A hand came down on Travis's shoulder as he started to turn away from the window. Nelson pushed back his derby and said, "I heard what that fellow said, Luke. You look a little upset."

"I was anxious to get to Cheyenne. Still am," Travis replied tersely.

"Must be important business taking you there. But I've traveled a lot, and I've learned that you can't get too upset at delays like this. They're going to happen, no matter what you do. The best thing is to take advantage of them." Nelson started steering Travis toward the street door of the depot. "Now, I happen to know this place where a man can get the best steak west of Kansas City. . . ."

Travis was relieved to learn the Sugar Loaf Café was

only two blocks from the depot. He would have no trouble hearing the whistle of the northbound train when it arrived. He also promised himself he would keep an eye on his watch.

Nelson led the way down the sidewalk toward the café. Denver's streets were paved, and its large, impressive stone and brick buildings gave the city a cosmopolitan look. But Travis knew that just beneath the polished surface lurked the brawling frontier town that had been only partially tamed by Marshal Dave Cook.

Located on the edge of the red-light district that was concentrated on Holladay and Larimer streets, the Sugar Loaf was in a two-story brick building. Travis and Nelson pushed through the double front doors and stepped into a smoky, low-ceilinged room with a bar that stretched the length of one side.

"Don't let the looks of the place fool you," Nelson said. "It may be a saloon, but the food's just fine."

Even at this early hour the saloon was crowded, and men stood two deep at the bar. Judging from the way they were dressed, Travis gathered that most of them were railroad workers and miners. He spotted a few cowboys among them.

The tables scattered around the room were also full. Painted women in gaudy, low-cut dresses served drinks and sat at some of the tables, laughing and flirting with the patrons. Occasionally one would lead a customer through a door at the rear of the room. Travis figured that an outside staircase led up to the rooms on the second floor where the establishment's other main enterprise took place.

Three miners got up from one of the tables near the bar and staggered toward the front door. They were obviously drunk, and one of them bumped against Travis as he left with his companions.

Nelson said, "Let's get that table," and moved quickly to do so. Travis took the chair opposite him.

A few moments later one of the bar girls sauntered to the table. "What can I do for you, gents?" she asked lazily.

"Two beers," Nelson replied. "And fry us up some steaks. Mashed potatoes, red beans, and deep-dish apple pie to go with them. Got that?"

"Sure, mister," the girl said. Then, eyeing Travis suggestively, she added, "Anything else?"

Travis shook his head. The girl shrugged, smiled, and sashayed back to the bar to relay the order to the bartender, who pushed open a door behind him and called the order to the cook.

Nelson grinned. "You're in for a treat, Luke."

Travis nodded somewhat absentmindedly. This dive was not the kind of place he normally patronized, and besides that he was still upset over the delayed train. But he made himself listen as Nelson told him about a previous trip to Denver. The man seemed to have been to a lot of places in the West, although he claimed that he had never visited Cheyenne before.

The girl brought their beers, and then a few minutes later returned with the platters of food. Nelson attacked his dinner with gusto. Travis ate with a little less enthusiasm, but he had to admit that the meal was surprisingly good. He would have enjoyed it more if he had not had to put up with the constant uproar coming from the Sugar Loaf's customers.

Suddenly some instinct triggered a warning in Travis's brain. He glanced up and saw two men standing at the bar, peering intently at the table where he and Nelson sat. They were not looking at him, however; their gazes were fixed on Nelson.

Nelson had taken off his derby and put it on the table beside his plate. He was relishing his food and paying no attention to what was going on around him.

The men at the bar abruptly became aware that Travis had noticed them, and they looked away to concentrate on their drinks. The marshal turned his attention back to his plate but kept a cautious eye on the men. They were both young and dressed in dusty range clothes, as if they had just ridden in from somewhere. Each man carried a pistol holstered in a tied-down rig on his hip. They were either handy with their guns or wanted folks to think they were. Travis hoped they were not looking for trouble. He was in no mood for it.

A few minutes later the two men gulped down their drinks, turned away from the bar, and started pushing through the crowd toward the table where Travis and Nelson sat. Travis put down his knife and fork when he saw them coming.

Both men looked grim and determined as they strode over to the table. Nelson still appeared not to notice them, but then one of the hard-faced men said harshly, "I know you, mister."

Nelson glanced up. "Are you speaking to me, sir?" he asked politely. His words were spoken so softly that they were almost inaudible in the tavern's hubbub.

"Damn right I'm talking to you!" the man shot back. "Ever since you came in here, I've been trying to remember where I saw you before, and it finally came to me just a few minutes ago."

He paused. Nelson put down his knife and fork, looked up at the man for a moment, and then shook his head. "Sorry, friend," he said. "I don't believe we've ever met."

"We didn't meet, but I saw you, all right." The man's lip curled in a hate-filled sneer. "You're the son of a bitch who hung my brother in Omaha last year!"

Travis glanced at Nelson, his eyes narrowed in surprise at this unexpected accusation.

Nelson did not answer the charge immediately. Moving deliberately, he lifted his napkin from his lap, wiped his mouth, and placed it on the table. "I did some work in Omaha last year," he said slowly. "I'm afraid I don't remember your brother, but if I hanged him, then he had a fair trial, was convicted by a jury, and sentenced by a judge. All I did was carry out the legal sentence." While Nelson spoke softly, his voice was edged with steel.

Travis was shocked by the revelation, but he worked to remain calm and controlled.

"You self-righteous bastard!" spat the man who had accused Nelson. "Here's where I even the score!"

The man's hand dropped to his gun, and his companion also started to draw. They were fast; Travis saw that instantly.

But P. K. Nelson also moved with surprising speed. His hand scooped up the platter of food in front of him and hurled it at the gunman who had spoken. The heavy plate, still laden with food, smashed into the man's face as he drew. He cried out involuntarily and staggered back, clawing at his gun.

Nelson rose out of his chair, his arm sweeping around in a backhand blow that caught his opponent on a jaw smeared with mashed potatoes. The impact jerked the man's head around. His gun came out of its holster, but he could not hold it. It slipped from his fingers and clattered to the floor.

In the same split second, Luke Travis surged to his feet, his hand flashing toward his gun. He saw that the second man was going to clear leather first. He had no time to be fancy.

Travis fired a shot from his hip. The other man might have gotten his gun out faster, but Travis's weapon was the first to roar. The slug slammed into the man's midsection, doubling him over and knocking him back. As he toppled, his gun barrel dropped. The pistol blasted, but the bullet thudded harmlessly into the floor at his feet. Then the man collapsed.

The first man was also crumpled on the floor, knocked out cold by Nelson's punch. Travis held his gun at the ready as he moved around the table to check on both of them. The man he had shot was dead, and the other one would not wake up soon. The marshal glanced at Nelson and saw that he was holding a short-barreled Smith & Wesson .38, popularly known as a "Baby Russian."

"You won't need that," Travis said. "This fight's over."

Nelson nodded curtly and stowed the pistol away in a holster that was clipped to his belt and concealed beneath his coat. Travis made a mental note of it and chided himself for not noticing the gun earlier. That showed how distracted he had been during this journey. Obviously P. K. Nelson was not a drummer as Travis had thought.

When the fight started, the patrons of the Sugar Loaf had lunged for cover. Now they began scrambling up off the floor and crawling from under tables.

No one seemed particularly upset by the violence. Shoot-outs such as this one, while not as common as they used to be, were still regular occurrences in Denver.

Travis slipped his Colt back in its holster and called to the bartender, "You'd better send for the sheriff."

"No need to do that, mister," a new voice called from the doorway. "You and your friend yust stay still."

Travis looked over his shoulder and saw a thick-bodied man with a white walrus mustache coming into the room. The newcomer wore a suit and carried a shotgun. His hat was pushed back on his bald head, and a badge was pinned to his vest.

A grin spread across Travis's face. "Take it easy, Olaf," he said. "Point that shotgun somewhere else before it goes off."

"Yah, and if it goes off, it'll be where I mean to point it," Sheriff Olaf Qualen said. "Is that you, Luke?"

"That's right," Travis said, turning around to face his fellow lawman. He stuck out a hand. "It's been a long time, Olaf."

Qualen shook hands with Travis, glanced at Nelson, and said, "What happened here?"

The noise level in the saloon was rapidly returning to its normal roar. Travis jerked his head toward the door, and Qualen, Nelson, and he stepped out of the saloon onto the boardwalk.

Once outside, Nelson said, "I guess it's my fault, Sheriff. One of those men recognized me and had a grudge to settle on account of his brother." He filled in the details of the fight.

"What are you doing here, Nelson?" the sheriff asked. His voice still retained a slight accent from his days as a boy in Norway. "We got nobody to hang right now."

"I'm just passing through. Our train was delayed, so I thought I'd show Luke where to get a good meal."

Qualen looked from Nelson to Travis. "You two traveling together?"

"More like just heading for the same place," Travis said. His eyes were narrow and thoughtful as he looked at Nelson. He could not help but think about what he had discovered in the last few minutes.

Qualen nodded. "I'll talk to the bartender, yust to make sure everything is straightened out. You two can go back to your supper."

"I'm afraid mine is all over the floor," Nelson said.

"And I've lost my appetite," Travis added.

"Yah, that can happen after a shooting." Qualen nodded as he led the way back inside.

The sheriff quickly questioned the bartender and some of the witnesses. Then, satisfied that Travis and Nelson had acted in self-defense, he ordered the dead man taken to the undertaker's. The other man was pulled to his feet and marched groggily out of the Sugar Loaf. He would be held for trial on charges of attempted murder.

Travis was quiet until Qualen had gone, then he said to Nelson, "I think I'll go back to the station to wait for the train. Like I told Olaf, I've lost my appetite."

"You and the sheriff seem to be old friends," Nelson commented.

"Acquaintances," Travis said curtly. "We're in the same line of work."

"Seems like there are some things you didn't tell me about yourself, Luke."

"That's true for you, too." Travis turned on his heel and stalked out of the Sugar Loaf.

The marshal stormed toward the railroad station. A moment later, Nelson caught up with him and fell in step beside him, clearly determined to ignore Travis's wish to be left alone.

"Look," Nelson said, "what Qualen and that hardcase said about me is true. I'm a hangman. A traveling executioner, I guess you could say. And there's no one better at his trade, I might add."

Travis glanced over at him. "You sound proud of it."

"And why shouldn't I be?" Nelson demanded. "My job is perfectly legal and all too necessary. I sometimes wish it wasn't."

"And now you're going to Cheyenne on business," Travis said icily.

"That's right." Nelson's voice was solemn as he went on. "I'm supposed to carry out the sentence of the court on a woman named Ruth Carson."

Travis stopped at the entrance to the depot and faced Nelson. In a flat, emotionless voice, he said, "Ruth Carson is my sister-in-law."

Nelson stared at Travis's stony face for a long moment, then finally said, "Oh. I—I didn't know. I'm sorry, Luke. I guess you're on your way to see her."

"I'm on my way to see that it doesn't happen."

Nelson nodded. "You're a lawman, aren't you?" he asked after a few seconds.

"I'm the marshal of Abilene, Kansas," Travis replied tautly.

"Then we're on the same side of the law, Luke," Nelson said quietly but firmly. "I'd like us to keep it that way, even if we don't see eye to eye on this. You know I have to do my job, just the way you have to do yours."

While Travis saw the man's logic, he was too furious to care. "That may be the way you see it," he said coldly. "But I'll tell you one thing, Nelson. When we get to Cheyenne, you'd better stay out of my way."

Without another word, Travis pushed past the hangman and went into the depot to wait for the northbound train.

Chapter Three

———

Luke Travis might have thought Cheyenne was a pretty place if he had been in the mood to appreciate such things. The rapidly growing settlement was situated in a basin on the eastern edge of the Laramie Mountains, which, while not as imposing as the Rockies beyond, were still quite majestic to someone who was accustomed to the rolling plains of Kansas.

Two hours after dawn, the train clattered over the trestle spanning Crow Creek and then chugged to a stop a few minutes later at the depot. The northbound had arrived in Denver earlier than was expected the night before, and its crew raced the locomotive through the night to make up the delay.

Travis had not seen P. K. Nelson boarding the train in Denver, and when he chose his seat, he made certain that Nelson was not in the car. Nelson did not seek him out, either, and Travis concluded that their harsh exchange had convinced the hangman to leave him alone.

Once again, Travis had not slept well during the night. As he disembarked, he realized that his muscles ached and his eyes were as gritty as if someone had thrown sand in them. He paused on the platform and rolled his shoulders to loosen them.

Then he walked quickly along the train to the baggage car to claim his bag from the clerk. As he turned to leave the platform, he almost ran into P. K. Nelson. He, too, had come to retrieve his bag.

"Good morning, Luke," Nelson said evenly.

Travis nodded but said nothing. He strode past Nelson into the depot building, walked straight through it, and emerged on the street.

The bustling streets of Cheyenne spread out before him. Men on horseback and wagons drawn by mules and oxen filled the dusty avenues. Most of the buildings had wide plank boardwalks similar to the ones in Abilene, although not as well constructed, and people thronged on them. Cheyenne was clearly a thriving city.

Travis knew that the discovery of gold in the Black Hills in nearby Dakota Territory had spurred the tremendous growth. It seemed as though every second man he saw on the street was dressed as a miner. They brushed shoulders with an equal number of cowhands, which made sense to Travis since he knew there were numerous ranches in the area. Cheyenne's rail depot was a vital supply link for both the miners and ranchers.

Stepping off the depot's porch, Travis started walking down the street and a minute later stopped one of the passersby. "Say, mister, can you tell me where to find the sheriff's office?" he asked.

The man was dressed in range clothes, but they were a little more expensive than those a regular cowhand could afford. Travis took him for a rancher. The man nodded and said, "Sure. Go a couple of blocks and turn left. You'll see it."

"Thanks," Travis told him. As he resumed his long stride, he began to wonder who the sheriff was these days. His old friend Jeff Carr was an officer in the State Militia now, although Carr still primarily ran down rustlers and assorted outlaws. Wild Bill Hickok had also enforced the law here but stayed only a short time before moving on to Deadwood. Travis grimaced at the thought. Hickok had been dead almost a year now, in some respects the victim of his own legend.

Travis turned the corner and on his left saw the sheriff's office, housed in a substantial stone building. Next to it stood an even sturdier-looking structure that no doubt served as the jail. He moved toward the office and opened the door.

He grinned, as the familiar room almost made him feel at home. A battered desk flanked by two wooden chairs stood in the center of the room. Behind it was a cabinet full of rifles and shotguns. Along one wall was a crumbling sofa that was losing its stuffing. A wood-burning stove with the ubiquitous coffeepot on it occupied a far corner.

Behind the scarred desk was a man sitting in a swivel chair who looked up as Travis's booted feet stepped heavily into the room. He had iron-gray hair and piercing blue eyes. Leaning back in his chair, he asked, "Can I help you, mister?"

"Are you the sheriff?" Travis asked.

The man stroked his narrow mustache as he nodded. "Will Dehner."

"My name's Luke Travis. I've come to see one of your prisoners."

The sheriff tensed and began to assess Travis. After a moment, he said, "I've got only three prisoners right now. Two of 'em are in here for guzzling too much whiskey and starting a brawl. You don't look like the kind of fella who'd want to see them."

"I'm talking about Ruth Carson," Travis said bluntly.

Dehner nodded. "Figured you were." He sighed and stood up. "Mind if I ask what your business is with her?"

"I'm her brother-in-law."

The sheriff was silent as he turned that over in his mind. Then he said, "I seem to recall hearing your name somewhere before, Mr. Travis. What line of work are you in?"

"I'm the marshal of Abilene, Kansas," Travis replied levelly. He had not heard of Will Dehner, but Cheyenne's lawman struck him as competent. There was something about him that said he could be as hard as nails when he needed to be.

Dehner nodded again. "Sure, I remember now. You say you're related to Ruth?"

"That's right."

The sheriff turned and yanked a ring of keys from a nail on the wall behind him and said, "Come on. I'll be glad to let you talk to her. She's in the back. We've got one cell here in the building, and I wasn't going to put her in with those drunks next door."

Travis was glad to hear that Dehner had some

compassion. During this ordeal Ruth had probably been treated decently. But he still refused to believe there was any reason why she should be in jail, no matter how well she was being treated. There had to have been some horrible mistake.

Dehner opened a door at the rear of the office and led Travis into a short hall. A single, sparsely furnished cell was on his left. On one wall was a bunk with a thin mattress and a gray blanket. A ladderback chair stood beside it. There was also a rocking chair in the cell, but whether it was a regular fixture or had been brought in especially for this prisoner, Travis did not know.

The woman in the cell was sitting in the rocking chair, but she stood up quickly as Travis entered the hall behind Dehner. A smile formed on her lips as she hurried toward the iron bars. "Luke!" she called softly.

Travis stepped toward the bars. "Hello, Ruth," he said. He started to reach for the hands she thrust through the bars when the sheriff stopped him.

"Marshal," he snapped, "I'd appreciate it if you'd unstrap that gun and hand it to me before you start visiting."

Travis glanced over his shoulder and saw that Dehner's hand was resting on the butt of his pistol. "Don't worry, Sheriff," he said as he unbuckled his gun belt and held it out to the lawman. "I'm not here to pull off any jailbreaks."

Dehner nodded as he took Travis's gun. "I'll let you two folks have a little privacy," he said. He went out and shut the door behind him.

How private that actually was, Travis did not know.

Dehner could easily listen through the door. However, the man did not strike him as the type to do that.

"Oh, Luke, it's so good to see you," Ruth said, grasping his hands and squeezing them hard. "I've been praying ever since I asked Kenneth to send that telegram that you'd come."

"Of course I came," Travis said gruffly as he searched Ruth's face. Except for a few strands of gray in her dark brown hair and a few lines around her intelligent brown eyes, she had not aged at all since he last saw her. Ruth Carson had always been a handsome woman. She still was. Good looks ran in her family, Travis thought, seeing Sarah in Ruth's finely molded features. The resemblance was so striking that the pain, which had once overwhelmed him, threatened to surface again. But Travis quickly suppressed it and went on. "Why don't you tell me what the blue blazes you're doing in jail?"

Ruth's welcoming smile was quickly replaced by a look of bitter resignation. "I've been found guilty of murdering a man," she said. "And the judge sentenced me to hang."

Travis shook his head. "You wouldn't hurt anybody."

"The jury decided differently, Luke. They say I poisoned Cheyenne's mayor, a man named Yates." Ruth's voice took on a mocking tone. "The Honorable Roland T. Yates, as he liked to be called. He was as honorable as a snake, Luke!"

Travis glanced around and spotted a three-legged stool standing in a rear corner of the hallway. He said, "Maybe you'd better back up and start at the beginning, Ruth. I've got to know what's going on if I'm going to get you out of this."

"Is that why you came, Luke?"

"Why else?" Travis drew up the stool and sat on it. "I don't intend to see an innocent person hang, especially not you."

Ruth pulled the rocking chair closer to the bars and eased into it. A smile curved her lips as she said, "Considering some of the run-ins we've had, I'm a little surprised you came all this way to help me."

Travis grinned. "Shoot, we just liked to fuss a little back and forth. It didn't really mean anything, did it?"

"I can see now that it didn't." Ruth took a deep breath. "You know I came here to start a newspaper."

Travis nodded. "As I recall, you said that any territory with the good sense to allow women to vote wouldn't mind a newspaper being edited and published by a woman."

"I still believe that's true. I ran into a few problems getting started, but no more than anyone does with a new business. The paper was finally doing well . . . then the election came up."

"Election?" Travis asked.

"Wyoming Territory does more than allow women to vote, Luke," Ruth said. "The laws also give us the right to hold public office. I decided to run for mayor."

At first Travis was surprised, but as he reflected on it, he knew he should not be. Ruth had always done the unexpected. "You ran against this Yates fella?"

"That's right." Ruth nodded. "He had served for two terms already, and to me that seemed long enough for one man to be in power. Besides, I wasn't fond of the way Yates ran the town and his business. I thought a change was necessary."

"But Yates won anyway," he guessed.

Ruth shrugged. "I did my best, but Yates was an experienced politician. He knew how to tell people what they wanted to hear. I only knew how to tell the truth." She got up and began to pace nervously. "The election campaign got rather ugly. Yates and I had had a lot of run-ins in the past."

"Like you and me," he suggested.

She shook her head. "Not at all, Luke. You and I were just snapping at each other. These were more serious. Yates and I disagreed on just about everything—from the way the town was run to its place in the territory. When he did something I didn't think was right, I took him to task in the newspaper."

Travis remembered how sharp Ruth's tongue could be when she thought she was right. "I'll bet that made him real fond of you," he said dryly.

She smiled. "He reacted exactly as you'd expect. Yates wasn't accustomed to anyone opposing him. He and his partner, a man named Flint McCabe, have always had things their own way here. I thought they had too much power. It goes to a man's head."

"Sometimes it does," Travis agreed. "This McCabe, you said he was Yates's partner?"

"That's right. Yates and McCabe owned a great deal of the town and quite a bit of property in the area. Yates ran the mercantile store they started, while McCabe was in charge of the big ranch north of here. Between them they controlled a sizable portion of the business in this part of the territory."

"And probably wanted more," Travis grunted. He had encountered before the type of man Ruth was describing.

"Naturally. I think that Yates and McCabe believed

that eventually they would run all of Wyoming. They already had enough influence to persuade the Territorial Legislature to do almost anything they wanted."

"But I imagine you fought them every step of the way."

Ruth had been pacing restlessly as she talked. Now she stopped and turned toward Travis, and he saw her brown eyes flash. "This is a wonderful place, Luke! It's some of the best ranching country I've ever seen. But there's room for farms and industry and the kind of development that could make Wyoming a good place to live for everyone, not just for big ranchers and businessmen. More and more people have come out here since the rail lines opened up, and the area is going to continue to grow. It can't grow properly if it's under the thumb of men like Yates and McCabe."

Travis nodded. He understood the way Ruth felt. Throughout the West men had grabbed for power and wealth, and the resulting struggles had spilled too much blood and caused more than enough pain. Yet he could see nothing wrong with a man trying to do his best for himself and his family. *Civilization,* he thought.

Ruth grasped the bars of the cell and leaned against them with a sigh. "I finally got tired of fighting with Yates, Luke. I really did. I'm not sure I was doing any good at all. After I lost the election, the people who supported me in the campaign were hurt. Yates was a man who held grudges, and he saw to it that my supporters were punished. He managed to run several stores out of business, and my lawyer lost clients. It sickened me to see that happen."

The more she said, the more Travis saw Ruth had a reason for wanting Roland T. Yates dead. But even given the situation, he still could not imagine her taking a man's life. "What did you do next?" he asked.

"I tried to make peace with him. I thought I might be able to do more good in the long run by working with Yates than against him." She laughed humorlessly. "It was a mistake, of course. I invited him to dinner at my house to show that I had no hard feelings . . . even though deep down I still despised him."

Travis did not like the sound of that. "Did Yates accept the invitation?"

"Of course. I'm a good cook, Luke. You know that."

He smiled. "I sure do. I remember that peach cobbler you made for Sarah and me when you visited us in Wichita—" He shook his head to banish the thought of Sarah and Wichita. "Go on," he said.

"Yates wasn't going to turn down a free meal. I put a provision on it, though, and he accepted. He had to listen while Malcolm and I made a few suggestions about how Cheyenne's affairs should be run. Strictly a friendly discussion, you understand. By that time I had had more than enough of the bickering."

"Who's Malcolm?"

"Malcolm Ebersole, my assistant at the paper." Ruth smiled. "He's a young man who used to be a reporter in Philadelphia. He decided to move out here in hopes of eventually having a paper of his own. I had those same dreams for so long, Luke, that I couldn't resist helping him. He's very sharp, and he's going to go far."

"Did he have dinner with you and Yates?"

Ruth shook her head. "No, he just sat in on the discussion and then left so that Yates and I could be alone." She blushed suddenly, and Travis suspected he knew what was coming next. Ruth went on. "Even though we had been enemies, I think Yates was always, well, interested in me. He was a widower; his wife had died before I came to Cheyenne. I believe he thought he could bring me around to his way of thinking."

"I don't imagine there was any chance of that, though."

"Of course not," Ruth said firmly. "As I said, I despised the man. But I was prepared to be civil, even polite. We sat down, had our dinner, and tried not to talk about the things we disagreed about. It was not . . . totally unpleasant. After dinner, I gave Yates some brandy, and then he left. On his way home, he became quite ill. He pulled his buggy to the side of the road and collapsed." She took a deep breath. "He died there: They found him sometime later that night."

Travis was silent for a long moment, then he said, "I suppose a doctor looked at the body."

Ruth nodded. "Of course. Our local doctor is a fine physician, a man named Stone. He examined Yates and found that the mayor died of poisoning. He wasn't able to determine exactly what kind of poison killed Yates, but there was no doubt that Yates *had* been poisoned."

"That doesn't mean that you were the one responsible," Travis said.

"No, but it was widely known that Yates had had dinner at my house that night. Sheriff Dehner asked around and learned that I had bought some rat poison at one of the mercantiles a few days earlier. That was enough to point the finger at me."

Travis rubbed his jaw thoughtfully as he considered

what she had told him. "That doesn't mean a thing," he said after a moment. "Plenty of people buy poison and have good reasons for it."

"That's true. I had what I thought was a good reason. We've been plagued recently with rats around the newspaper office. That's why I bought it."

As anger began to grip him, Travis stood up and stalked back and forth. "You mean to tell me you were found guilty on *that* evidence?"

"It was a bit circumstantial," Ruth agreed, "but it was enough for the jury. They knew about my feud with Yates, knew I had bought the poison, knew Yates was dead." She nodded solemnly. "Yes, Luke, it was enough."

"Not for me, dammit," he growled. He stopped pacing and peered intently at Ruth. "Did you kill him?"

She met his gaze levelly and shook her head. "I swear to you that I didn't. I was honestly trying to make peace with Yates, even if he was an arrogant blowhard. I didn't kill anyone."

For the first time Travis saw tears shining in her eyes and heard a slight quaver in her voice. He stepped closer to the bars. "I'm sorry I even asked, Ruth," he said gently. "I knew you were innocent."

"You know it, and I know it, Luke, but that won't stop me from hanging for the crime in a few days."

Travis reached through the bars and, putting his hands on her shoulders, squeezed tightly. "I'll stop it," he promised. "I'll find out who really killed him. You're not going to hang, Ruth."

She rested her hands on his arms and leaned her cheek against his sleeve. The intimacy made him a little uncomfortable, but he did not move. Ruth was upset and had good reason to be. "Thank you," she said softly. "I knew you'd come and help me. I just knew it."

"Don't you worry about a thing," he said, trying to console her. "I'll get to the bottom of this." He took her chin in his hand and lifted it, and a thought occurred to him. "What about that rancher McCabe that you mentioned? If he was Yates's partner, it looks to me like he might have just as much reason to kill him as you. More, really."

Ruth shook her head. "McCabe was nowhere near town on the night Yates died, and he can prove it easily. No, I'm really the only one who had an opportunity to kill him. All I know is that I didn't do it."

"Maybe the best opportunity, but not the only one," Travis told her. "We don't know how long it took for the stuff to work. Somebody could have slipped it to Yates before he got to your house. For that matter, how do you know that he didn't stop somewhere after leaving your place?"

Ruth nodded thoughtfully. "That's true. I suppose it could have happened that way. But how are you going to find out, Luke?"

A grim smile played over his lean face. "This mess is like an anthill, Ruth. I'll just poke a sharp stick in it, stir it around a bit, and see what comes running out."

"You can get stung that way," she replied with a smile.

"Not if I move quickly enough," he said, grinning.

Chapter Four

———◆———

LUKE TRAVIS SPENT A FEW MORE MINUTES REASSURING Ruth Carson that he would do everything in his power to get her out of this predicament, then told her good-bye for the time being. He went to the door that led into the office and found it locked. A knock on the panel quickly brought Sheriff Dehner, who opened it. Travis lifted a hand in farewell to Ruth and then followed the sheriff into the office.

"Find out what you wanted to know?" Dehner asked as he closed the door.

"I found out enough to make me mad," Travis replied flatly. "You *know* that woman in there didn't kill anybody."

The sheriff shook his head. "That's not what the jury said, and they have the final word. I just do what the law tells me to do."

Dehner was unconsciously echoing what P. K.

Nelson had said earlier. Travis felt a surge of anger, but he restrained it and said, "I'll want to look at the records of Ruth's trial."

"That's fine. You'll have to talk to Judge Shaw about that, but I don't imagine he'll have any objection." Dehner sat down and placed his hands flat on the desktop. "Listen, Marshal, I know you're upset about your sister-in-law, and I can understand it. But I can tell you this. Judge Shaw has been on the bench for years. He knows what he's about. There was nothing illegal or irregular about her trial. It was as fair as it could be."

Travis ignored his statement. "When did you arrest her? How soon after Yates died?" he asked sharply.

Dehner shrugged. "The next morning, as soon as I found out that she had bought rat poison. Doc Stone came by early that morning and told me what killed Mayor Yates. Up until then, nobody was sure that he hadn't keeled over from natural causes. That poison made it murder."

"And you didn't investigate anybody except Ruth Carson, did you?"

"Who else was there to investigate?" Dehner asked, spreading his hands. "The man was poisoned. He had dinner with a woman he'd been feuding with for years. Seems like a pretty simple case to me."

Travis leaned over the desk and looked intently at the sheriff. "Before this happened, would you have believed that Ruth Carson could kill anybody?" he asked.

Dehner hesitated for a long, uncomfortable moment, then frowned. "Well," he said reluctantly, "maybe I wouldn't have. She always struck me as a lady who'd speak her mind, maybe too much so, but I didn't figure her for a killer." He shook his head. "But that doesn't mean she didn't do it. Folks do things all the time you'd never figure them for."

"What about other suspects?" Travis snapped. "Surely there were other people with a reason to want Yates dead."

"There might have been some hard feelings on the part of some of the citizens. The mayor was a successful man, and you don't get that way without making a few enemies."

"And what about this Flint McCabe?"

Dehner snorted in disbelief. "He was the mayor's business partner."

"That's right. Didn't he profit by Yates's death?"

"That's hard to say. In his will the mayor left everything to his daughter. Of course, McCabe has more control now, even if he doesn't own any more than he did before. A young woman can't run things like her father would have, and she'll have to rely on McCabe." Dehner leaned forward in his chair. "But McCabe has an alibi. He was out at his ranch, nowhere near town. He couldn't have poisoned Mayor Yates, and he wouldn't have wanted to. You can take my word, Travis, those two got along fine. They had come a long way together, and they were going to keep going, too. In another few years, you wouldn't have been able to find two more important men in the whole territory."

"That's what Ruth told me. And now McCabe's got all that to himself."

Dehner shook his head. "You're on the wrong trail, Marshal." He stood up. "Just what is it you intend to do while you're here in Cheyenne, anyway?"

Travis looked at him levelly. "I intend to find out who really killed Yates."

"That case is closed." Dehner's tone carried a clear warning.

"Not to me," Travis replied coldly.

The sheriff lifted a hand and pointed a finger at his visitor. His other hand was resting on his gun butt. "Don't get out of line in my town, Travis," he said. "You may be a lawman back in Kansas, but you have no jurisdiction here in Cheyenne. Just remember that, and whatever you do, stay inside the law, you understand?"

Travis stared at him for a moment, then nodded abruptly. "I intend to," he said. At least for as long as he could, he thought.

Ruth had said her lawyer's name was Kenneth Blanchard and had given Travis directions to his office, which was a block and a half from the jail. As he left, he turned over in his mind what Ruth had told him. He was hoping the lawyer could suggest a starting point for his investigation. Eventually, he knew he was also going to have to find a place to stay. He was still carrying his bag. At the moment, though, Ruth's problem was a great deal more urgent.

As he started down the street, Travis spotted P. K. Nelson coming toward him. The hangman recognized Travis at the same time, hesitated briefly, then came resolutely along.

The marshal noticed that Nelson was not carrying his bag, and he concluded that the hangman must have checked into the hotel already. Now he was probably on his way to see Sheriff Dehner. Travis glanced down the street beyond Nelson and saw the massive stone courthouse looming up ahead with a large grassy area in front of it.

That's where the gallows will be built, Travis decided. Nelson must have been looking the place over.

Not trusting himself to speak, Travis clamped his lips tightly together and averted his eyes. Neither man spoke as they passed each other on the boardwalk.

Kenneth Blanchard's office was on the second floor of a whitewashed frame building above a bakery. An outside staircase led up to the attorney's chambers. As Travis climbed the stairs, the fragrant aromas that wafted from the bakery reminded him that he had not eaten any breakfast before leaving the train. At the time he had not felt like eating, but the smell of fresh bread made his stomach rumble.

At the top of the staircase was a small landing and a single door. A neatly lettered shingle read KENNETH BLANCHARD—ATTORNEY-AT-LAW. Travis knocked on the door, then tried the knob. When it turned easily, he shrugged and stepped inside.

A man was sitting at the desk with his arms propped on the desktop between neat piles of paper and his chin resting in his hands. There was a look of weariness and despair on his face as he stared down at the papers that were piled so high they threatened to overwhelm him. He heaved a heartfelt sigh, then glanced up at Travis. "What can I do for you, mister?" he asked in a voice noticeably lacking in enthusiasm.

"Are you Kenneth Blanchard?" Travis asked.

"That's right."

The marshal strode to the desk and extended his hand. "My name is Luke Travis. I'm Ruth Carson's brother-in-law."

Blanchard stood up hurriedly and shook Travis's

hand. "Well, Mr. Travis," he said with a smile, "it's good to meet you. I know Ruth has been looking forward to your arrival. Have you talked to her yet?"

"I have," Travis replied grimly. "She told me about what happened with Yates and her trial."

Blanchard wagged his head. "A nasty business, thoroughly unpleasant."

The lawyer was a small man with graying brown hair, a neat mustache, and spectacles perched on the bridge of his nose. His coat was off, but he wore a vest and tie. A large bookcase lined with leather-bound legal volumes occupied most of one wall. Except for the paper-cluttered desk, the office was as fastidious as Blanchard himself appeared to be.

"I've come to talk about the case," Travis said, "and to see if we can come up with anything new on it, Mr. Blanchard. Is that all right with you?"

"Of course, of course." Blanchard waved at the chair in front of the desk. "Have a seat, Mr. Travis. Or should I call you Marshal Travis?"

"Make it Luke," Travis said as he sat down. He was not particularly impressed with Blanchard, but he did not want to alienate him. He had a feeling he was going to need all the allies he could find in Cheyenne.

"All right, Luke. What can I tell you about the case that Ruth hasn't?"

"How strong was the evidence against her?"

Blanchard sighed. "Strong enough for the jury to convict her. There was no doubt that she bought the rat poison. Several reliable witnesses testified to the purchase, and for that matter, Ruth never denied it."

"What happened to the poison?" the marshal asked. "Wasn't Ruth able to account for it?"

"She had already used it," Blanchard replied, shaking his head. "The way it was spread around the newspaper office, there was no way to tell if any of it had been used for . . . other purposes."

"Like murder," Travis said bleakly.

"Yes," Blanchard sighed. "Exactly. I tried to point out to the jury that the burden of proof was on the prosecution. While I could not prove that Ruth didn't use the poison on Yates, the prosecution could not prove that she had." The lawyer sighed again. "Obviously, I didn't do a good enough job to convince them."

"What about the other folks who might have wanted Yates dead?" Travis asked. "Did you point them out?"

"I tried to, but the prosecutor objected that such a line of speculation was irrelevant to this case. The judge sustained the objections every time. He said that Ruth was on trial, not anyone else."

Blanchard's mouth twisted in contempt. "Meaning Flint McCabe, of course."

Travis nodded. "Then you thought about him, too."

"Certainly. Anytime a man dies under mysterious circumstances, you have to suspect his business partner. I said as much to Sheriff Dehner. Evidently he had already questioned McCabe, because he said he had a solid alibi." Blanchard shook his head. "I'm sorry, Luke. I did everything I know how to do for Ruth. It just wasn't enough."

The regret in Blanchard's voice was genuine, Travis sensed, and the feeling was mirrored in the man's eyes. Nor did he doubt his honesty or sincerity, and from the sound of things, his competence was not in question, either. He realized that visiting Judge Shaw and going over the transcript would waste time—

valuable time he did not have. The deck had just been stacked too heavily against Ruth. Now it was up to Travis to find out who had done the stacking.

"What now?" he asked. "Do you have any plans to try to stop this hanging?"

"I've sent a wire to the territorial governor appealing to him for clemency or at least a stay of execution. I haven't received a reply yet, but I don't expect much help from that source. Ruth's editorials were very critical of the governor. I'm sure calling him a tool of the big ranchers didn't endear her to him." Blanchard gave a short, bitter laugh.

Travis got to his feet. "I don't intend to let her hang, no matter what she wrote," he said flatly.

"But . . . what can you do? You're a lawman, you know you can't stop a legal execution."

That question had already begun to nag at Travis. He had spent years upholding the law. Even though he was completely convinced of Ruth's innocence, if he was unable to prove it in time, what could he do? Would he be capable of pulling off a jailbreak to rescue her? That would mean going on the run, leaving behind his job and all of his friends in Abilene.

Maybe it won't come to that, he thought. "I've got a few days. We'll see what I can come up with in that time."

"I hope it's enough, Luke. I pray that it is." Blanchard stood up and moved from behind the desk to shake hands with Travis again. "If there's anything I can do to help, please let me know."

"I will." Travis gave in to his curiosity and asked, "You're not from around here, are you?"

Blanchard smiled. "I'm originally from Connecticut. My doctor in Hartford advised me to come west for my health. The fresh air would do me good, he said. I have to admit he was right. Until this business with Ruth came along, I was feeling like a new man."

Travis nodded. "The frontier is better for most folks than they expect it will be. I'll see you around." He paused in the doorway and looked back at Blanchard. "Where is Ruth's newspaper office?"

"One street over and a block west," Blanchard told him. "You'll see the sign. It's called the *Cheyenne Eagle.*"

"That's a good name for her paper," Travis said with a grin. "The eagle is a good fighter. So is Ruth."

She would need to be, he thought, considering the trouble she was in.

He picked up his bag and left Kenneth Blanchard's office. When he reached the bottom of the stairs, Travis paused for a moment, then went to the door of the bakery. *Maybe something to eat would stimulate my brain and start me thinking more clearly,* he decided. A few moments later, he emerged from the establishment chewing on the soft, fresh doughnut in his hand.

As he followed Blanchard's directions and walked toward the newspaper office, he studied the people who passed him on the street. They were generally a little rougher looking than the citizens of Abilene, but that was to be expected since Cheyenne was farther west and had been settled more recently. He was sure it would be a fine place to live eventually, but for the time being, it was still a little raw around the edges.

Travis spotted the office of the *Cheyenne Eagle* in a one-story frame building wedged between a saddle shop and a dry-goods store. A painted sign on the overhang above the boardwalk depicted an eagle in flight above a mountain peak. The words of the newspaper's name flanked the majestic bird on each side. *It's a striking sign,* Travis thought.

As he crossed the street toward the newspaper office, he could see activity inside through the big plate glass windows on either side of the open door. Through the doorway floated the clanking sound of machinery, and Travis realized as he stepped onto the boardwalk that the press was running. Despite the fact that its editor was in jail, the *Eagle* was still being printed.

Travis paused in the doorway and looked the place over. The strong smell of ink permeated the air. Several tables littered with paper were scattered around the big room. In the rear stood the massive press, making its loud, insistent racket. Beside it were big rolls of paper.

The two men in the office wore ink-stained aprons. One of them turned the crank on the press while the other stood by watching the printed sheets come out. The one who was overseeing the printing operation must have sensed Travis's presence, because he turned around to see who had entered the office. Since he was standing next to the clattering press, there was no way he could have heard Travis's footsteps.

The man smiled and came toward Travis. Raising his voice to be heard over the din, he called, "Hello! Is there something I can do for you?"

He was young, no more than twenty-five, with a shock of sandy hair and a bit of a lantern jaw. His eyes were brown, and the gaze they fastened on Travis was intelligent. He was handsome in a rawboned way.

"You must be Malcolm Ebersole," Travis said.

"That's right." The young man wiped his hand on

his apron and then thrust it toward Travis. "Have we met?"

"No. My name is Luke Travis. I'm Ruth Carson's brother-in-law."

Ebersole pumped Travis's hand. "Luke Travis!" he exclaimed. "This is quite an honor. Ruth told me all about your exploits as a lawman."

Uncomfortable with Ebersole's enthusiasm, the marshal shook his head. "I just try to do my job," he said. "But I'm not here as a lawman now; I'm just somebody who's worried about Ruth."

Ebersole nodded, and a solemn expression replaced the grin. "We're all worried," he said. "It doesn't seem possible that she's going to be . . . well, it's just not right. Ruth never tried to hurt anybody."

"That's the way I figure it," Travis agreed. "I don't know who killed this Mayor Yates, but I'm sure it wasn't Ruth."

The young newspaperman nodded. He turned to the press and called to the man operating it, "You're doing a fine job, Simon. You just go right ahead. This gentleman and I will be in the office."

The man at the press nodded and kept cranking. He was even younger than Ebersole, Travis noticed, a stocky youth who was barely out of his teens.

Ebersole led the way around the press to a door that opened into a small office. A cluttered old desk and a couple of wooden chairs were the only furnishings in the tiny room except for a bookcase, the shelves of which bulged with volumes. Travis glanced at the titles and saw everything from the classics to a book of stories by a writer from back east named Poe. Travis had read some of the man's work in a book that Aileen Bloom loaned to him, and although they had been a little strange for his taste, he felt sure that Ruth would like them. She always enjoyed things that were out of the ordinary; that trait was probably what led her into newspaper work.

Ebersole sat down behind the desk and waved Travis into the other chair. "What can I do for you, Marshal?" he asked. "If you're here to help Ruth, I'm completely at your disposal. If she's executed, it will be a hideous miscarriage of justice."

"That's the way I feel," Travis agreed. "Who do you think really killed Mayor Yates?" he asked bluntly.

The young man shook his head. "I don't have any idea. All I know is that Ruth didn't. Hell, Yates had enemies all over the territory."

Travis cocked a booted foot on his knee. "Most men in these parts settle their disputes out in the open," he said. "They use a gun or a knife or their fists. You won't find many men who'll use poison."

"That's true enough." Ebersole laughed shortly. "Just in the relatively short time I've been out here, I've seen probably half a dozen gunfights. Why, just a few months ago Charlie Harrison and Jim Levy shot it out in front of Frenchy's Saloon. It made quite a story for the paper."

"I've heard of Levy. Gunman from Nevada, isn't he?"

"That's right." Ebersole nodded. "And Charlie came from back east somewhere. He had killed several men himself, but he won't put any more in their graves. He's there himself now."

"What about Yates?" Travis asked. "Anybody ever try to call him out?"

Ebersole laughed again and shook his head. "Mayor Yates was not skilled with a gun, and everyone knew it. He never even carried one. Now, his partner Flint McCabe is a different story. I've never seen him in action, but he's fast, or so I've been told."

"He doesn't sound like the kind of man who would use poison on his partner."

"Not at all. Besides, I always thought McCabe and Yates got along better than most partners. I can't imagine McCabe trying to kill the mayor."

"Maybe not. But I've got to start somewhere. I intend to find the real killer."

"You've only got five days to do it," Ebersole warned grimly. "Less than that, really, since the judge set the time of the hanging for nine o'clock in the morning."

Travis grimaced. He was all too aware of the time limit.

Suddenly he realized that the clanging had stopped, and the press had gone silent. A moment later there was a soft knock on the office door. Ebersole called, "Come in," and the young man who had been operating the press stuck his head inside.

"It's all done, Mr. Ebersole," he said. "Do you want to come check on the papers?"

"I'm sure they're fine, Simon. We'll let them dry, then get them out on the street, all right?"

"Sure, Mr. Ebersole." The young man bobbed his head. He glanced shyly and curiously at Travis.

"Marshal Travis, this is Simon Smith," Ebersole said. "Simon has been helping Ruth and me around here. He's just learned to run the press, haven't you, Simon?"

The youth nodded again and grinned. "That's right, Mr. Ebersole," he said happily. Travis sensed that he was a little simpleminded, but he seemed pleasant enough and eager to please. Simon went on. "I'm glad to meet you, Marshal."

Travis stood up and shook hands with him. "Same here, Simon. I'm Miss Carson's brother-in-law, and I appreciate you pitching in here at the paper." He glanced at Ebersole. "I imagine Ruth insisted that you keep publishing the paper."

Ebersole laughed. "You know her pretty well, don't you? That was one of the first things she said to me after she was arrested. 'I don't want you missing a single issue,' she said, and she meant it. So Simon and I have been trying to live up to her expectations. Simon, get one of the papers for the marshal."

Simon ducked into the outer room and came back waving one of the printed sheets. The ink was still a little wet. Travis took it and said, "Thanks. I've got to go find a place to stay, so I'll take the paper with me." He reached into his pocket for a coin and handed it to Ebersole over the young man's objections. "This paper's still a going concern," Travis insisted. "Ruth will want it to stay that way until this mess is cleared up."

"Do you honestly think it will be, Marshal?" Ebersole asked anxiously. "Is there a chance we can still save her?"

"There's always a chance," Travis declared. "As long as I'm alive, Ruth Carson's not going to hang."

Chapter Five

———◆———

LUKE TRAVIS FOUND A PLEASANT, DECENT HOTEL A COUple of blocks from the town square and checked in. He requested and received a room on the second floor overlooking the street. The Barnes Hotel was not fancy, but the bed in his room seemed comfortable when Travis sat down on it for a moment. It certainly beat a blanket roll on the trail.

He did not take the time to unpack. Instead, he stowed his bag in the room, locked the door behind him, pocketed the key, and went down to the lobby. Once there he strode to the desk and asked the clerk, "Where would I find Mayor Yates's house?"

The man behind the desk looked startled. He glanced at the register to remind himself of the guest's name, then said, "Why, Mr. Travis, I'm sorry to tell you this, but Mayor Yates has passed away. I hope you didn't have business with him."

Travis shook his head. "No, and I wasn't his friend. Never met the man. But I assume his daughter still lives in the same place."

"That's right. It's over on Grantham Street." The clerk quickly told Travis how to find the late mayor's house, then asked, "Do you have business with Miss Penny, Mr. Travis?"

"I just need to talk to her for a few minutes," Travis replied. Nodding his thanks to the clerk, he went out to the boardwalk and turned west as the man had directed.

As Travis walked down the street, he wondered if the clerk would tell Sheriff Dehner of his request. He had a feeling that the sheriff kept a pretty close eye on what happened in his town.

Travis passed the square on his way to the house that now belonged to Penny Yates. He noticed P. K. Nelson coming out of the courthouse, accompanied by several men in work clothes. A wagon loaded with timbers and planks stood in the street nearby.

The sight made Travis grimace. He knew that Nelson and the workmen were about to begin construction of the gallows. He vowed to himself that the apparatus would not get any use.

He easily found the Yates house. Surrounded by a manicured lawn, the large whitewashed frame structure sat on a slight rise. A long veranda swept around the front of the house, and several spired cupolas adorned the steep roof above the second floor. It was an impressive house, the kind of place where a wealthy, influential man would live.

Travis opened the gate in the wrought-iron fence that enclosed the lawn, followed the stone walk to the porch, and climbed the steps. Rapping sharply on the door, he stepped back to wait, and a moment later he heard the patter of footsteps inside. As the door swung open, he reached up and swept off his hat.

A slender young woman looked up at him. She was in her early twenties, Travis judged. Her thick, cornsilk blond hair fell to her shoulders and framed a face that was undeniably lovely. She appraised him with flashing blue eyes.

"Yes?" she asked. "Can I do something for you?"

"Are you Miss Yates, ma'am?" he asked.

"That's right. I'm Penny Yates."

"My name is Luke Travis, Miss Yates. I'd like to talk to you for a few minutes, if I might."

"Does this concern a business matter?"

"More of a personal matter," Travis replied.

Penny Yates considered for a moment, then nodded and stepped back to open the door the rest of the way. "Come in," she said politely.

Travis stepped into an ornately appointed foyer. Penny moved around him and gestured to him to follow her into a parlor that opened up to the right. A large oak desk piled with papers stood against one wall of the opulently furnished room. Filling the wall opposite it was a huge fireplace with a massive mantel. Gauzy curtains were drawn over the windows, subduing the light that filtered into the room. Travis thought it was appropriate, considering that the owner of this house had died not long ago.

Penny's dark, sedate dress was further evidence of the recent death, but even in mourning clothes, she was beautiful. She turned to face Travis and said, "Please have a seat, Mr. Travis. Would you like some tea, or perhaps something else?"

He shook his head as he sat down on an expensively upholstered sofa. "No, thank you, Miss Yates."

Penny settled into a brocaded wing chair. "Well, then, what can I do for you? What is this personal matter you wanted to discuss with me?"

"It's about your late father, ma'am," Travis said bluntly. "I'm Ruth Carson's brother-in-law."

Penny's breath hissed between her even white teeth. Anger flared in her eyes as she said, "Then I'll thank you to leave my house, please, Mr. Travis."

"I really need to talk to you, Miss Yates," Travis said without making a move to get up.

"I have nothing to say to any relative of that . . . that murderess!" Penny snapped. "Please leave."

Travis was not accustomed to ignoring a lady's request, but this was too important to let good manners interfere with finding out what he needed to know. "Miss Yates," he said firmly, "I'm just trying to get to the bottom of this and find out who really killed your father. I would think you'd want to know that, too."

"That woman killed him," Penny shot back. "Everyone in town knows that. Surely you can't claim now, after she's been tried and convicted, that she didn't do it?"

"That's exactly what I think," Travis told her. "I know Ruth Carson, Miss Yates. She's perfectly capable of carrying on the feud with your father that she told me about, but not of killing anyone. She's sworn to me that she's innocent, and I believe her."

"That doesn't mean a thing." Penny's voice was as hard as stone, harder than seemed possible coming from a young woman with lush blond hair and creamy skin. "The jury said she was guilty, and the judge sentenced her to hang. That's all that matters."

"Is that what you want?" Travis asked softly.

"I want justice," Penny snapped. "My father is dead, and Ruth Carson has to pay for that."

"Even if she's innocent?" Travis prodded.

"She's not." The young woman sounded absolutely convinced.

Travis hesitated a moment, then asked, "Miss Yates, have you ever seen anyone being hanged?"

"Of course not," Penny replied. "My father never allowed me to watch such a thing. But I intend to witness this execution."

Travis nodded. Then his voice grew harder as he said, "Then I'll tell you what you're going to see, Miss Yates. The person being hanged usually has his hands tied behind his back. In this case, *her* back. The hangman will put a black hood over Ruth's head and then place the noose around her neck while she stands on the trapdoor of the gallows. When it drops, her weight will hit the rope, and the jerk will break her neck—if she's lucky. If she's not, she'll hang there until she strangles. It can take a long time. It's an ugly sight, Miss Yates."

Even though the images he conjured up hurt him, Travis spoke in a rush, bearing down on the ugliness of it as he tried to get through to Penny Yates. But although he saw her flinch a time or two at the harshness of the scene he described, the resolve in her face did not falter.

"There's nothing I can do to stop this execution, Mr. Travis," she said when he was finished. "And even if there were, I wouldn't want to. Ruth Carson killed my father." She shook her head. "I can't feel sorry for her. Now, I believe I asked you to leave several minutes ago."

Travis ignored her last statement. "Isn't there anyone else who might have wanted to see your father . . . well, out of the way?"

"You mean dead, don't you?" she said in a deliberately harsh voice. She stood up and walked to the window, peering out through the curtains at the street. Travis saw her shoulders move and knew that she was trying to regain control over emotions that threatened to overwhelm her. When she turned around to face him, her face was composed. She said calmly, "My father was a prominent businessman in this territory, Mr. Travis, and besides that he was a politician. He was a powerful man."

"So I've been told."

"A man does not achieve that success without making some enemies along the way. There will always be people who don't understand. . . ."

Penny was saying the same thing everyone else in Cheyenne had told him. Roland T. Yates *had* made enemies.

Travis leaned forward and said intently, "Is it so hard to believe that one of your father's other enemies might have been responsible for his death?"

"It is when you consider the evidence," Penny replied. "He went to dinner at that woman's house and then he . . . he died. What could be plainer, Mr. Travis?"

Travis could not argue with the young woman's logic. If he had not been personally involved with the case, he probably would have believed Ruth was guilty, too. But he knew better, and he would not quit prodding.

"What about your father's business partner?" he asked. "What about Flint McCabe?"

At that moment, the front door of the house opened, and a man stepped into the foyer in time to hear Travis's last question. He stopped short, a frown forming on his face, and snapped, "What *about* Flint McCabe?"

Travis stood up, turning to face the newcomer. The man was tall and lean, with a dark, handsome face. He wore range clothes, but they were clean and showed little wear. His black Stetson was pushed back on his head, revealing crisp dark hair. A Remington .44 revolver rode in a well-oiled holster on his hip.

The man took a step into the room. "I asked you a question, mister. What were you saying about Flint McCabe?"

Penny hurried over to him. "It's all right, Flint," the lovely blonde said quickly. "This gentleman was just leaving. Weren't you, Mr. Travis?" She turned and glared at the marshal.

Travis studied Flint McCabe for a moment before he answered. He was fairly young, probably in his midthirties. After hearing about the man's influence and successful running of the ranch Yates and he had owned, Travis had expected McCabe to be older.

He ignored the look that Penny Yates gave him and said, "My name is Luke Travis, Mr. McCabe. I'm Ruth Carson's brother-in-law, and I've come to Cheyenne to look into this matter."

McCabe glanced down at the young woman and put a hand on her shoulder. "Has this man been bothering you, Penny?"

She shook her head. "He just had a few questions he wanted to ask about . . . about my father's death."

"So I heard." McCabe looked back at Travis. "You weren't suggesting that I might have had something to do with what happened to Roland, were you, Travis?"

"I was just asking Miss Yates's opinion. You were her father's business partner, after all."

"I was just about to tell him how insane it is to think that you had anything to do with it, Flint," Penny declared. "I know that you and Father were friends as well as partners."

"That's right." McCabe started to move past the girl, but she reached out and put a hand on his arm to stop him. Looking at Travis, he went on. "We don't need you coming around here and causing trouble, Travis. What gives you the right to bother people like Penny here?"

"Like I told you, I'm Ruth Carson's brother-in-law," Travis replied grimly. "And I'm also the marshal of Abilene, Kansas. As a lawman, I'm interested in seeing justice done."

McCabe seemed taken aback by Travis's pronouncement, but he recovered quickly and tightened his jaw. Slipping an arm around Penny Yates's shoulders in a proprietary manner, he said, "That doesn't matter. You don't have any authority here in Cheyenne, mister, and I don't want you bothering the woman I'm going to marry."

Travis was surprised by the sudden revelation. But it made sense. According to the theory Travis was developing, McCabe could strengthen his control over what went on in this territory only by marrying Penny.

But when Travis looked at Penny Yates, he saw an uncomfortable expression in her eyes. Her breathing had quickened when McCabe embraced her. As Travis studied her now, he came to the conclusion that her reaction was not one of pleasure or excitement.

Penny did not contradict McCabe's statement, though. Instead, she said, "Please, Mr. Travis. I've asked you several times now to leave me alone. I don't want any more trouble. I've had quite enough of that lately."

"Don't worry, Penny," McCabe assured her as he tightened his grip on her. "I'll see that this fella doesn't bother you anymore." He put his other hand near the butt of his Remington and stared angrily at Travis. "You leaving?"

Travis took a deep breath and reined in his own temper. Losing it now would not accomplish anything except maybe to get him thrown into Sheriff Dehner's jail. As he had been told more than once since he arrived in Cheyenne, he had no authority, no jurisdiction, here.

"I'm going," he said. McCabe and Penny moved aside as he left the parlor and went into the foyer. He paused there and looked back as he put on his hat. "You may not believe this, Miss Yates, but I am sorry about your father."

"I . . . Thank you, Mr. Travis." Penny said nothing else, and her tone made it clear that she expected Travis to leave immediately.

The marshal turned and went out the door. He could feel McCabe's eyes boring into his back as he went down the walk and turned toward the downtown area of Cheyenne. It was an uncomfortable sensation, and Travis had the feeling that McCabe wished he were studying him over the sights of a rifle. He was going to have to watch his back while he was in Cheyenne.

But that was not unusual. Luke Travis had had plenty of men gunning for him. Somehow, though, he had never gotten used to it enough to like it.

Flint McCabe probably would not try anything, Travis decided. The man did have to think of his position in the community. But there was an unmistakable ruthlessness in the man's face. Travis was certain that a great deal of McCabe's success was due to that trait.

Travis found a small café and went inside to order some lunch. The waitress brought him a platter of pork chops, mashed potatoes, and beans. He enjoyed the meal, despite everything that was on his mind.

As he stepped onto the sidewalk after he had finished eating, he suddenly heard the sound of hammering. He stopped and winced as he realized that the pounding was coming from the square.

Nelson and his men were at work already, Travis thought. The hangman was not wasting any time. He had been in Cheyenne only a few hours, but the gallows were already under way.

Travis shook his head. He could not afford to waste time being angry with Nelson, but he could not quite banish the disappointment he felt. He had liked the burly hangman—before he found out what his line of work was.

"Marshal!"

Travis turned to see who had hailed him. Sheriff Will Dehner was striding purposefully down the boardwalk toward him. His grim expression showed that he meant business.

"Hello, Sheriff." Travis nodded as Dehner walked up to him. "What can I do for you?"

"You can stop bothering the citizens around here. That's what you can do," Dehner snapped.

Figuring out who had complained was easy. Travis knew that Kenneth Blanchard and Malcolm Ebersole would not have gone to the sheriff upset about his conversations with them, so that left only two possibilities.

"Who came to see you, Sheriff? Was it McCabe or Miss Yates?"

Dehner chewed his mustache for a moment, then said, "If it's any of your business, McCabe is the one who lodged the complaint. He said you'd been over at Miss Penny's house pestering her."

"Did Miss Yates come along to back up that claim?"

"She didn't have to," Dehner growled. "McCabe's not going to lie to me, Travis. He has some respect for the office of sheriff."

Having met McCabe, Travis doubted that, but he did not waste his breath arguing with Dehner. Instead, he asked, "Did McCabe file an official complaint?" He was almost hoping that the rancher had. That would force Penny Yates to tell her story to the sheriff if Dehner tried to make the charge stick.

From the look in Penny's eyes as McCabe embraced her, Travis had a feeling there was a limit to how far she would go to back him up.

However, Dehner shook his head. "Mr. McCabe said he didn't want to cause you any more trouble than he had to. He just wanted me to have a talk with you, to see if you'd back off and stop causing a commotion about this."

Travis's voice hardened. "I think Ruth Carson's life is worth raising a ruckus about, Sheriff. And I'd like to know why the simple act of asking a few questions has McCabe so worried if he has nothing to hide."

Dehner started to reply, then stopped abruptly, as if the logic of Travis's comment had just sunk in. The moment did not last long, though. "It's my job to ask the questions around here, Travis," he said curtly. "I'm satisfied. The judge and jury were satisfied. All that remains is to carry out the sentence of the court. Now, you've got a right to stay here in Cheyenne until that's over. But I don't appreciate you coming into my bailiwick and trying to stir things up. I want you to stop disrupting my town."

"What's more important, Sheriff?" Travis snapped. "Keeping things running smoothly for you or learning the truth? It's starting to sound to me like you're in Flint McCabe's pocket."

Dehner's face flushed with rage, and Travis tensed for the lawman's reaction. He knew how he would feel if someone came into Abilene and accused him of being paid off. But his frustration was beginning to get the better of his common sense.

The sheriff made a visible effort to control his anger. "I'm going to try to forget you said that," he growled, "since I know how upset you are about your sister-in-law. But what I said goes. You leave folks alone, or you'll find yourself behind bars." With that, Dehner turned and stalked away.

As Travis watched him go, he became aware once again of the incessant hammering that had been in the background all during their conversation. It seemed so loud that he doubted he could go anywhere in Cheyenne and not hear it. Like the ticking of an unnaturally loud clock, it would serve as a constant reminder of just how little time he had left to save Ruth's life.

It was going to be up to him alone, Travis knew. Dehner was not going to make any effort to reopen the investigation into Yates's death. Blanchard and Ebersole wanted to see Ruth cleared, of course, but neither man was the type to take things into his own hands.

No, he was in this by himself.

Chapter Six

TRAVIS SPENT THE AFTERNOON FAMILIARIZING HIMSELF with Cheyenne, visiting several stores and a few saloons. Along the way, he picked up as much gossip about Mayor Yates's death as he could from clerks and bartenders, most of whom were eager to talk about the murder. The townspeople who overheard his conversations were only too happy to volunteer their comments, so that by early evening he had a good idea what the town thought.

Most of the citizens seemed to agree that Ruth had indeed poisoned Yates, although many of them thought it was a shame she had been caught at it. Travis discovered that despite his victory in the last election, Yates had not been a particularly well-liked man. The inhabitants of Cheyenne had wanted to stay on Yates's good side, but not many had mourned his passing.

More than one person expressed disbelief that Ruth could have done such a thing, but nearly everyone admitted that the evidence certainly looked damning. Travis kept his opinions to himself, along with his true identity. He concentrated instead on drawing out the thoughts of the people he was talking to.

And wherever he went, he continued to hear the pound, pound, pound of the carpenters' hammers as they nailed together the gallows.

Travis returned to the café where he had eaten lunch to have his supper. The place was busier at night, and he had to wait awhile to be served a steak with all the trimmings. He followed that with a dish of excellent peach cobbler, but while he knew the food was good, he did not seem to taste much of it. He wondered if Ruth was being fed well in the jail.

That thought did away with the last of his appetite. He left a little of the cobbler, paid his bill, and walked out into the street. The sun had gone down a few minutes earlier. He saw the fading rosy glow in the sky and the quickly gathering shadows in the alleys between the buildings.

Glancing around, Travis oriented himself again and turned toward the jail. He wanted to make sure Ruth was all right and to let her know that he had started investigating the mayor's murder.

When Travis entered the office, he found a younger man seated in Sheriff Dehner's chair behind the desk. He had a deputy's badge on his chest and looked up at Travis from behind a pair of thick spectacles. "Hello," he said pleasantly. "Can I help you?"

"I'd like to see Miss Carson. My name is Luke Travis."

From the look on the young deputy's face, the name

clearly meant something to him. He frowned as he pushed back his chair and stood up. "Sheriff Dehner said you might come by. He told me to let you see the prisoner anytime you wanted."

"Tell the sheriff I appreciate that," Travis replied sincerely. If the situation had been reversed, he was not sure he would have been so cooperative.

The deputy plucked the key ring off the nail on the wall and opened the door into the little cellblock. Travis stepped into the hall leading past the single cell. Ruth was sitting in the straight-backed chair this time, eating from a tray that she had balanced on her lap.

"That cobbler looks familiar," Travis said with a grin. "They must bring your meals from that café down the street."

Ruth returned his smile. "One of the advantages of being in jail, I suppose," she said.

The deputy gestured with the ring of keys. "Did you want to go into the cell, Mr. Travis?" he asked.

"This is all right, son, thanks."

Ruth placed the tray on her bunk and stood up. "Luke, if you don't mind, I would like you to come in."

"Well, sure." Travis nodded. He slipped his Colt from its holster and extended it, butt first, to the deputy. "That's the only gun I've got on me, but you're welcome to check if you'd like."

"I've heard of you, Marshal," the young man replied as he took the Colt from Travis. "I'll take your word for it." He tucked the weapon behind his belt and then unlocked the cell door. "I'll leave you folks alone."

Travis waited until the deputy had retreated into

the office and shut the door behind him. Then he stepped into the cell and faced Ruth.

She moved into his arms, and he automatically reached out to embrace her. Her face rested against his chest as she drew a deep, shuddering breath.

"Thank you, Luke," she said in a voice that was little more than a whisper. "It's been a hard time, and I . . . I just needed to be held for a minute."

"Sure," Travis replied. "Sure. That's fine." He felt awkward and uncomfortable, unsure what he should do. He thought about patting her on the back, then rejected the idea. Instead, he just stood there, his arms loosely around her.

After a moment, Ruth sighed and lifted her head. As she stepped back she had a mocking smile on her face. "I think that's about all the intimacy two old adversaries like us can stand, Luke. But I do thank you for that."

"You're welcome," Travis said gruffly. "Why don't you sit down and finish your supper?"

"All right." She picked up the tray and sat down on the bunk. Reversing the straight chair, Travis straddled it. Ruth went on. "I do appreciate your coming to see me. Kenneth and Malcolm stop by fairly often, but they're so depressed, their visits usually just make me feel worse."

"They don't know what to do to help you," Travis said. "I'm not sure I do, either, but I'm going to give it a try. I went to see Penny Yates earlier today. Met Flint McCabe while I was there."

Ruth looked surprised. "Did you learn anything from either of them?"

"Not much." Travis shrugged. "McCabe and I

didn't get along too well. He struck me as a man who can be dangerous when he wants to be."

"He is," Ruth agreed grimly. "He runs the Trident spread with an iron hand. There have been rumors about some killings in his past, too."

"I can believe that. Trident, eh? That's the brand Yates and he used?"

"That's right. One leg of the trident for McCabe, another for Yates."

"Who's the third leg for?" Travis asked.

Ruth shook her head. "Penny, I suppose. Not that it really matters. Yates and McCabe were enough for anyone to have to deal with."

"Ran roughshod over anybody who got in their way, eh?" Travis grunted. "I can believe that after meeting McCabe. What *is* going on between Penny Yates and him?"

Ruth frowned. "The mayor was always hinting to Penny that McCabe and she should get married. I sensed that McCabe was willing, but Penny wasn't. Yates wanted his relationship with McCabe cast in stone, though, and I suppose he thought that would do it."

"Sounds logical." Quickly, Travis told Ruth about what he had seen at the Yates house. He added, "It looks to me like Penny changed her mind about marrying McCabe since her father's death. She has to be feeling pretty worried about what's going to happen to her."

"Of course," Ruth agreed. "Marrying McCabe might look like the best solution to her. Without him to run things, the estate she inherited from her father isn't going to be worth much."

"But with McCabe?"

"Then they're well on their way to their own little private empire," Ruth said solemnly. "Especially if they get married."

"McCabe doesn't have to share that power with anyone now," Travis mused. "Penny won't be a threat to anything he wants to do. I could tell she's not going to oppose him."

Ruth set her supper tray aside. "You still see McCabe as the most likely suspect, don't you, even with his alibi?"

"He had the most to gain by Yates's death. He could have hired somebody to help him with the actual murder." Travis narrowed his eyes and rubbed his jaw thoughtfully. "How did Yates and McCabe get started, anyway? I haven't heard anyone talk about that."

"I'm not sure," Ruth replied slowly. "They were here when I moved to Cheyenne. They weren't as successful then, but they were already building up their ranch." She frowned in thought. "Now that I think about it, their holdings seemed to grow pretty rapidly."

Travis leaned forward. "The quickest way to build up a ranch is to help yourself to another man's cattle. Do you think that's what McCabe did?"

Ruth shook her head. "I don't know, Luke. I just don't know."

"Might be worth looking into." Travis stood up. "I need more information, and the best place to find out what's really going on in any town is probably the red-light district."

Ruth smiled faintly. "Here in Cheyenne it's called the Golden Gate district. It's along Ferguson Street. You'll find practically everyone who's involved in anything shady over there." She stood up and lightly touched Travis's arm. "But you're not really going over there, are you? It's a robbers' roost, Luke. Sheriff Dehner won't go into that part of town unless he has to, and then he brings several deputies with him."

"Don't worry about me." Travis grinned. "I've dealt with some pretty unsavory characters in my time."

"But if those men over there know you're a lawman—"

"I don't plan to tell them," Travis cut in. "I'll be fine, Ruth. And I'll wager that I'll find somebody who can tell me a little more about Mr. Flint McCabe and his activities."

With the grin still on his face, he stepped out of the cell, closed the door behind him, and went over to the cellblock door to summon the young deputy.

By the time Travis left the jail, the evening's festivities in the Golden Gate district were already well under way. Travis found it without any trouble just by listening to the uproar coming from the saloons that lined Ferguson Street.

The hammering on the gallows had finally stopped for the day, and Travis was glad of that. The noise had gotten on his nerves and made him so edgy that he had trouble thinking straight.

As he strode along the street, he glanced into the saloons that he passed. The entrances and windows framed scenes of drinking, laughing, and carousing. Music from pianos and fiddles floated in the night air; the different tunes blended into a discordant melody that was occasionally punctuated by a shrill cry.

So far, Travis had heard no gunshots. *It must be a quiet night,* he reflected.

Across the street, Travis saw an establishment that took up an entire block. It was a two-story frame structure with a long sign attached to the railing around its balcony. STUBB'S PLACE, the sign declared; smaller letters beneath read *Restaurant, Bar, Rooms for Rent.*

From what Travis saw through the windows, the bar occupied the entire first floor. Shapes cavorted by lantern light, and he could hear a band playing. Quite a few horses were tethered at the hitchrack in front, and there was a steady stream of men coming and going through the batwings.

It looked like a good place to have a drink and maybe collect some information, Travis thought as he started across the street. He had to wait for a couple of wagons to rattle by, then climbed onto the boardwalk and stepped to the saloon's entrance.

Pausing just outside, Travis studied the big room a little more closely before he entered. The bar ran the length of the back wall, underneath an interior balcony. Staircases led up to the second floor on both sides of the room. Stuffed animal heads adorned the walls. Travis saw deer and antelope and even the head of a huge silvertip grizzly. As he swung his gaze around the room, he blinked when he saw a buffalo head. The buffalo seemed to be staring down malevolently at the men and women below him, as if offended that it had to witness such goings-on.

A grin tugged at Travis's mouth as he stepped into Stubb's Place. The Golden Gate district was a remnant of the wild frontier town Cheyenne had been only a few years before, and Stubb's appeared to be a vivid example of that legacy.

He had taken just a few steps inside the door when something tapped him on the shoulder. Travis looked around in surprise, then glanced up and let his eyes follow the long pole that had nudged him.

To one side of the door, five feet above the sawdust-covered plank floor, was a raised platform supported by heavy beams. On the platform stood a chair that was occupied by a man wearing a dark suit. The man's feet barely touched the platform, Travis quickly noted before he spied the sawed-off shotgun lying across the man's lap.

When he saw that he had Travis's attention, the man leaned the pole against the wall and then patted the stock of his weapon. "Just wanted to let you know I've got me eye on you, mate," the man said in a gravelly voice that easily carried above the music and laughter blaring in the room.

"Do you always greet customers that way, friend?" Travis asked.

The man had brawny shoulders and thinning dark hair and appeared to be in his forties. "I do when they be strangers," he said. "Me name is Montgomery Stubb, mister, from Liverpool, England. And I don't stand for trouble in me place. Understand?"

For a moment, Travis's mouth tightened. It seemed as though everyone in Cheyenne delivered warnings, and he was getting tired of it. But then he forced himself to grin and replied, "I'm not here looking for trouble, Mr. Stubb, just a drink of good whiskey."

"Then you've come to the right place." Stubb slid from the chair, cradling the shotgun in his arms. He gestured with its barrels toward the bar. "The first one's on me. Just tell the bartender."

Travis nodded. "Thanks." He turned and started to make his way among the crowd toward the bar. Halfway across the room, he glanced over his shoulder and saw Stubb standing on the platform, his dark eyes surveying the room. As Travis had thought, the man was not tall, only a little over five feet. Stubb fit his name. But there was no mistaking the fact that he was in complete command of this place, nor that he would be a dangerous man to cross.

Travis found a spot at the bar, shouldered his way between two rough-looking men dressed in dusty range clothes, and lifted a hand to catch the barman's eye. One of the cowhands beside him growled a curse as Travis told the bartender, "Whiskey. Stubb said the first one was on him."

The barman nodded and splashed liquor into a glass. Travis was not expecting high-quality whiskey, and what he got was typical bar whiskey, raw and watered down.

He cast a hard-eyed glance at the man next to him, who was still muttering about being moved aside. The cowboy quieted down as Travis glared at him. Then Travis turned to use the long, gilt-framed mirror behind the bar to study the saloon's patrons. Many of them were cowboys, but there were a few townsmen and railroad workers. Bar girls in lacy, low-cut dresses moved among the men. Narrow-eyed gamblers flipped cards on the green felt tabletops. Men who wore their guns tied low on their thighs sat watchfully nursing their drinks. *Hardcases*, Travis thought. Above them all sat Montgomery Stubb, the master of the hall, who ruled with a sawed-off shotgun.

The marshal was glad his badge was stowed safely away in his pocket. A known lawman would be taking quite a risk coming in here alone.

Travis took a deep breath and then tossed off the rest of the whiskey, trying not to grimace as it burned fiercely in his throat and stomach. He thumped the empty glass on the bar and gestured to the bartender to refill it. Rolling a coin to the barkeep, he picked up the fresh drink and turned to start back across the room.

He had to dodge several dancing couples along the way, but a moment later he was standing beside the platform where Stubb sat. Grinning up at the short saloonkeeper, Travis said, "Thanks for the first one." He lifted the second drink in a brief salute.

"You're welcome," Stubb said as he leaned forward. "Enjoy yourself, friend."

"Oh, I intend to. But I would like to ask a question, if you don't mind."

Stubb frowned. "We're not much on questions around here, mister. But seeing as you be new in town . . . what is it?"

"If you're the owner of this place, why are you acting as the bouncer?"

A grin split Stubb's homely face. "I like to keep me hand in, so to speak. I started out busting heads in a place back in Boston when folks got out of line. Guess I got in the habit."

"You look like a man who keeps a close eye on things," Travis said with a thoughtful nod. "You probably know everything that's going on in this territory."

"Maybe." Stubbs peered at him suspiciously. "What do you want to know?"

Travis sipped his drink. "I was just wondering what a man could do to earn a little money around here," he said lightly.

"You're in need of a job, are you?"

"We all have to eat," Travis answered with a shrug.

"What are you good at, me friend?"

Travis let his hand drift down to the butt of his gun. "This and that," he said.

Stubb nodded sagely. "I see."

Venturing a little further, Travis said, "I've heard there's been some trouble around here with rustling. I thought I might be able to help somebody who's been having problems."

Stubb cocked his head, and his tone grew harsh as he asked, "You're not a damned range detective, are you?"

Travis threw back his head and laughed. "Not hardly," he said.

"Well . . . a man in me position hears things. Just rumors, mind you. But if you're looking for someone who's been losing cattle, it seems to me you could talk to just about any rancher in the area."

Travis's eyes narrowed. "It's that widespread?"

"I wouldn't know who's behind it, mind you. I run an honest place here. What folks do outside these walls ain't none of me business."

Travis nodded. "Do you know a man named McCabe?"

"Everybody in this part of the country knows McCabe, mister. What's he to you?"

"I was just wondering if his ranch was being hit, too."

"Same as everybody else, from what I've heard." Stubb shook his head. "I'm a friendly sort, but I think this conversation has gone far enough. If you're here to drink, go right ahead. If you're just wanting to ask questions, you'd best go someplace else."

"Thanks," Travis said dryly. "I think I'll drink."

The marshal left after finishing his second glass of whiskey, though. As he pushed through the batwings, he could feel Stubb watching him, and he knew that the saloonkeeper was suspicious. He wondered if Stubb would tell anyone about the inquisitive stranger.

That was the beginning of a long evening for Travis. He visited several saloons along Ferguson Street and managed to talk to bartenders and patrons in each of them, always steering the conversation around to the rustling in the area. When he came to the Golden Gate district, he had not intended to become so involved in the problems the cattlemen were having, but all of the instincts he had developed in his years as a lawman told him that the questions might turn out to be important.

No matter whom he talked to, the story was the same. There was plenty of rustling going on in the territory, but the Trident ranch had suffered its share of losses. As for McCabe's background, no one was willing to come right out and accuse him of rustling when Yates and he had been starting up their ranch, but it was implied more than once.

A little before midnight Travis headed back toward his hotel. He had been nursing whiskeys and beers for several hours, and while he was not drunk, he did have a headache from the liquor. And he was frustrated because he did not know if he was any closer to finding out the truth about the murder that had landed Ruth in jail. At the moment, the best thing he could do was get some sleep. Maybe he would be able to think more clearly in the morning.

The bullet that came out of the darkness and slammed past Travis's head was so close that it sounded like the crack of a whip next to his ear.

He threw himself forward, grabbing for his Colt as he fell. Twisting around, he spotted the spurt of flame coming from a nearby alley as the hidden gunman fired again. The second slug smacked into the dirt of the street a couple of feet from Travis.

He jerked up his pistol and triggered twice, then rolled quickly to the side. There was no return fire, though. Travis surged to his feet and darted toward the building next to the alley. He flattened against its wall, putting himself out of the line of fire of anyone hiding in the shadows.

Travis stayed there for several long moments, watching the mouth of the alley. No one emerged, and there were no more shots.

No one seemed to be coming to investigate the gunfire, either. He supposed exchanges like this were not that unusual, especially ones of such short duration. Probably Dehner or one of his deputies would show up sooner or later to ask a few questions and try to find out what had gone on.

Travis did not want to be there when that happened. Apparently the gunman was gone now, driven off by Travis's shots, and the man from Abilene decided that he wanted to be gone, too. Still holding his gun ready, he moved across the street and hurried toward his hotel.

No one else bothered him or tried to ambush him. At the hotel entrance Travis finally holstered his gun. His racing pulse had slowed down after the brief flurry of violence, but the wheels of his brain were still whirling.

There were a number of reasons why someone would have taken a shot at him. It could have been something as mundane as an attempted robbery. Or it could have been that his questions had stirred someone up, just as he hoped they would.

Maybe he was closer than he thought to finding the real killer of Mayor Roland T. Yates.

Chapter Seven

EARLY THE NEXT MORNING, SHERIFF WILL DEHNER WAS at his desk when the door of the office swung open and P. K. Nelson strode in. Nodding to Dehner, the hangman said, "Good morning, Sheriff."

"Mr. Nelson," the sheriff replied. "What can I do for you this morning?"

"I was wondering if it would be possible for me to meet the prisoner."

Dehner leaned back in his chair and frowned. Nelson's request was an unusual one. If *he* were the executioner, Dehner reflected, he would not want to meet anyone he was about to hang.

Nelson had come to the office the day before and introduced himself. Dehner was expecting him, knowing that the judge had sent for the hangman. But the man's pleasant demeanor and habit of spinning yarns was a surprise. Dehner anticipated that a man in

Nelson's profession and with his reputation would be a grim individual.

Now the hangman wanted to talk to Ruth Carson, and although Dehner could not imagine why, there was no reason for him to deny the request. "Sure," he said as he pushed back his chair and reached for the keys. "Come on."

The sheriff led the way into the cellblock. Despite the early hour, Ruth had already had breakfast. She had placed the empty tray on her bunk and was sitting in the rocking chair, reading a copy of the *Cheyenne Eagle* that Dehner had brought to her.

"Have you come for the tray, Sheriff?" Ruth asked without glancing up from the paper.

"I'll take it," Dehner replied. "But I've got somebody here who wants to see you, Ruth."

Ruth looked up then, saw Nelson standing behind the lawman, and frowned. "Hello," she said to Nelson. "I don't believe we've met, sir."

"No, ma'am, we haven't," Nelson said, sweeping off his hat and stepping closer to the bars. "My name is P. K. Nelson, and I just wanted to say hello to you."

Ruth's eyes narrowed. "Have you come for the hanging, Mr. Nelson?"

Nelson's cheerful expression wavered, and his smile threatened to disappear as he said, "Well, I suppose you could say that, Miss Carson."

"Are you a journalist? Your suit reminds me a bit of some reporters I've known." Ruth's tone was dry and cynical.

Nelson shook his head. "No, ma'am. I'm an officer of the court." He shifted his feet nervously, and

Dehner could tell that Nelson did not want to admit to Ruth that he was going to be her executioner.

"I see. Well, then, I don't believe that we have a great deal to say to each other, Mr. Nelson." Ruth lifted her newspaper again in a gesture of dismissal. "Good day, sir."

Dehner looked at Nelson and jerked his head toward the office. The hangman nodded and went out. When the two men were back in the office and the door to the cellblock was closed, Dehner asked, "What the hell was that all about?"

"I'm sorry," Nelson said, and he sounded sincere. "I just needed to get an idea of the lady's weight and her, ah, build. Such things are important when you're designing a gallows. Now that the platform and steps are finished, I'll turn to the trapdoor mechanism."

Dehner snorted. "I thought a gallows was just a gallows."

"No, you're wrong there. Each gallows is different and must be adjusted to the person being hanged. I don't want any mistakes. That can be very bad. In fact, there's nothing worse than a gallows that doesn't work just right. It can take a long time for the sentence to be carried out to its conclusion."

"So you were just working when you went back there to talk to Ruth," Dehner stated coldly.

"I'm afraid so." An odd, distracted look came over Nelson's face as he went on. "But I wanted to meet the lady, too. I've never hanged a woman before, Sheriff. To be honest, I wasn't sure how I would react." He took a deep breath. "But I'll do my job, never fear. I just wish the lady had not been so attractive. That's distressing, quite distressing. . . ."

Nelson left the office muttering. Dehner stared after him for a moment, then shook his head and went back to the paperwork stacked on his desk.

At about the same time, Luke Travis left his hotel and strolled down the street to a livery barn he had noticed the day before. He knew he would have to do some riding and needed to rent a horse.

A young man was working at the stable, carrying hay into the stalls. Travis paused just inside the barn's big double doors and waited until the lad came out of one of the stalls. The young man saw him, put down his pitchfork, and came toward him with a grin. "Something I can do for you, mister?" he asked.

"I need a horse," Travis replied. "Do you have one I can rent for a few days?"

"Sure. How about this one right over here?" The stable lad went to one of the stalls and reached over the gate to pat the flank of a chestnut mare. "She's right friendly, and she'll get you anywhere you want to go."

Travis joined the lad at the stall. He studied the lines of the horse for a moment, then nodded in approval. "She'll do," he said. "She have a name?"

The youth grinned again. "We call her Baby."

A grimace tugged at Travis's mouth. Despite her name, the horse looked like a fairly good mount. She was young, healthy, and strong. He probably would not find a better one for rent. Quickly, the young man and he completed the financial arrangements, and Travis managed to get the use of a saddle thrown into the fee. He handed over the money, then watched while the young man led Baby out of the stall and saddled her.

"Take good care of her, mister," the lad said as Travis swung into the saddle. "We're right fond of her."

"I'll be careful," Travis promised. He heeled the animal to a walk and rode into the street.

He had not slept much after the attempt on his life. The shooting itself did not bother him too much—a man never got used to somebody throwing lead at him, but such incidents became less shocking as the years went by. Instead, Travis was occupied by what he had learned during his day of investigation.

Initially Travis had thought his questions had not turned up much of value. But if the person who tried to ambush him was connected with this case, then maybe he was more successful than he first assumed. Something he ran across was important and prompted the ambush. He just did not know how it all tied together yet.

The widespread rustling seemed to be the main piece of information he had uncovered. He was a little surprised to learn that McCabe had suffered losses.

When Travis had gotten out of bed that morning, he decided it was time to take a look around and familiarize himself with the lay of the land. He had been told the Trident ranch was north of town. While he did not know its exact location, he had heard it was so large that he would have no trouble finding it. If he headed north from Cheyenne, he would wind up on Trident range sooner or later.

That was exactly what he did, riding easy in the saddle and quickly leaving Cheyenne behind. The Laramie Mountains loomed to his left. The rugged heights of Pole Mountain were the highest point in this part of the range. To his right was the rolling prairie that gradually flattened out to become the Great Plains farther to the east. A few rocky gulleys scarred the terrain, but overall it was fine ranch land, Travis thought as he forded a rippling, tree-lined creek. Even though it was summer, a cool, gentle breeze blew off the mountains, and wispy white clouds floated high in the deep blue sky. He rode through the lush, fertile pastureland and had traveled less than ten miles when he began to spot cattle grazing.

Around midmorning, Travis steered Baby close enough to a small herd of cattle to read the brand on their flanks. It was unmistakably in the shape of a three-pronged spear—a trident. He was on McCabe's land.

McCabe's land . . . and Penny Yates's, as well, Travis corrected himself. He wondered how McCabe would react if the young woman decided to take an active hand in running the ranch. That was unlikely, Travis knew, but it was an intriguing idea.

He rode up a hill, topped it, reined in, and paused to look down on the rich green valley that spread out before him. Hedgerows outlined a creek that wound gently out of the foothills to the west. It was as pretty a place as Travis had seen in a long time.

Suddenly a rifle cracked to his right, and Baby surged forward as a slug burned a furrow across her rump. Travis leaned down and spurred her into a gallop.

Part of him had expected that whoever had shot at him the night before would try again, but the pleasantness of the ride through the Wyoming countryside must have dulled his senses, he thought angrily. He crouched low in the saddle as another shot whistled over his head. Several whoops and yells made him turn around to see four men riding out of a clump of trees, angling toward him in an attempt to cut him off.

"Come on, Baby," Travis hissed through clenched teeth. His keen eyes searched the landscape for some cover. The men were firing rapidly now. It was unlikely they would hit him, aiming as they were from the backs of galloping horses, but if they caught up with him, the odds would be too high. He would have to reach cover.

Travis prodded the mare westward toward the foothills. The terrain was rougher, and there was a greater likelihood of finding some protection near the creek. Luckily, the mare was running smoothly and well, and he was surprised at the speed she had at her command.

Sliding out his pistol, the marshal squeezed off a shot at the men pursuing him. He knew it was unlikely he would hit anything at this range, but at least the shot would let them know he intended to fight back. He did not shoot again, preferring to save his shells until they would have a chance to do some good.

Suddenly Travis spotted a group of small boulders up ahead on the shoulder of a little rise. He pointed the horse toward the rocks, then ducked involuntarily as a bullet whined close to his head. The four men were closer now, but he could tell that they would not be able to intercept him before he reached the boulders.

The odds were still discouraging—four against one, and they were armed with rifles while all he had was his Colt. But at least he would have a chance to put up a fight. Maybe he could do some discouraging of his own, make the price for taking him high enough that they would not want to pay it.

He had to drive them off. If they killed him now, Ruth would hang for sure.

Travis glanced over his shoulder to see how close the bushwhackers were, then hauled back on the reins as the mare reached the clump of rocks. The horse came to a sliding stop. Travis dropped out of the saddle, slapped the mare on the rump to start her running again, then threw himself behind the largest of the boulders. He had to crouch to get his body behind the rock. Stabbing the barrel of his pistol around the boulder, he triggered off three shots at his attackers.

They were close enough now to be within revolver range, and Travis's slugs made them rein in and hunt for cover of their own. The man from Abilene raised his head long enough to see them dismounting and running toward some small trees. They spread out as they ran, so that with their rifles they would be able to cover the whole hillside where Travis was holed up.

Travis thumbed fresh cartridges into his Colt to replace the spent ones. His pulse was pounding from the frantic ride and the danger in which he found himself. There was nowhere for him to go now. He was pinned down with a limited amount of ammunition, no food or water, and no possibility of help. No one knew he was out here, and he had no friends in Cheyenne to come looking for him.

Unless something extraordinary happened, he was going to die out here today. But he would not go down alone, he vowed as his grip tightened on the revolver in his hand.

He edged around the boulder again and snapped a shot toward the trees. As Travis's slug chewed a piece out of a tree trunk, a flurry of frantic movement behind another tree caught his eye, but he did not have time to see anything else. The other men opened fire, making him duck behind the rock.

Abruptly the rifles fell silent. A long moment passed, then Travis heard one man calling to the others. His words were clearly audible. "Wilt, you and Richmond head over that way. Try to flank the son of a bitch!"

Travis did not recognize the voice or the names, but that meant nothing. These men were probably hired guns or ranch hands who worked for McCabe.

If the men named Wilt and Richmond succeeded in getting off to his side, this fight would be over in a hurry. They would be able to pick him off while the other two kept him pinned down.

Travis twisted and leaned toward the other side of the rock. He had to hit the two men as they tried to flank him, even though doing so would probably expose him to the fire of the other pair. He spotted Wilt and Richmond as they darted from tree to tree and lifted his gun to venture a shot at them.

A bullet smacked into the boulder just above his head, and the impact sent dust and rock chips flying into his face. Travis dropped to one knee and blinked rapidly to clear the dust from his eyes. When he was able to look up, he saw he had missed his shot. Wilt and Richmond had taken cover in some trees on his flank.

They opened fire on him. Travis hunkered down as low as he could as bullets ricocheted off the boulder less than a foot from him. He tipped his Colt up and fired blindly toward the bushwhackers.

Suddenly he became aware that fewer bullets were coming in his direction. He glanced up and saw one of the men who had flanked him scurrying from behind the trees. The man turned as he ran and fired at something behind him. Then, abruptly, the man staggered, dropped his rifle, and clutched at his thigh. He stayed on his feet somehow and hobbled back toward the other two men. His companion joined him in fleeing, caught up to him, and grabbed his arm to help him along.

A flicker of movement over his left shoulder caught Travis's eye, and he turned to see what it was. A man on horseback was coming over the top of the rise about a hundred yards away from him. From that angle the man had a clear line of fire at all four ambushers. Travis poked his gun over the boulder and joined in the barrage that the newcomer was firing with a Winchester. The man was uncannily accurate, considering that he was galloping at a downhill angle. His bullets were coming close enough to drive the ambushers back to their horses.

Travis stood up and fired the last two rounds in his Colt as his attackers hurriedly mounted up and began to flee. The odds were still in their favor, Travis thought as he watched them gallop off, but now they were meeting more resistance, and they did not have the stomach to face it.

The lone rider sent two more rifle slugs screaming after them, then reined in his horse. He sat for a moment, watching until the four ambushers had disappeared, then turned his mount and rode slowly toward Travis.

The marshal looked around and spotted his horse about fifty yards away, dancing nervously at the top of a ridge. He started walking toward the mare, and when he got close enough, he began talking softly and soothingly to her. Baby cast a suspicious glance at him, but Travis was able to reach out and grasp the dangling reins. He patted the horse and checked the bullet burn on her rump. The wound did not appear to be serious. Travis led her back down the hill.

The stranger was waiting for him at the clump of boulders. He was twisted in the saddle, watching the spot where the four bushwhackers had vanished, just in case they tried to sneak up again. He grinned when he looked at Travis.

"Seems like I owe you some thanks, mister," Travis said. "They would have rousted me out pretty quick if you hadn't shown up."

The man reached up and pushed his hat back, revealing curly brown hair. "Didn't look like a fair fight to me," he said. "Didn't sound like it, either, from the other side of the ridge. That's why I rode up to take a look. My name's Joel Wray."

"Luke Travis," the lawman said. He reached up to shake hands with Wray. As he did so, he glanced at the man's horse and saw that it wore a Trident brand.

Joel Wray, a young man in his midtwenties, was wearing a faded blue shirt, jeans, and a battered black hat. His well-cared-for boots were worn. A Colt rode in a holster on his hip, and he still had the Winchester in his hands. From his outfit and the coil of rope that was hung on his saddle, Travis guessed that he was one of McCabe's cowhands.

"Mind if I ask what you're doing out here, Mr. Travis?" Wray asked. "You're on Trident range, and I don't recollect seeing you around before." The young man studied Travis suspiciously.

Travis did not blame Wray for being wary. If there was as much rustling going on as there seemed to be, then any stranger would have to have a mighty good reason for riding through this territory. "I'm glad I ran into you," he said. "I was looking for McCabe's spread."

"Well, you found it. You have business with McCabe?"

"I'm not sure." Moving slowly so as not to spook Wray, Travis swung into the saddle. He met Wray's eyes and debated just how much to tell the young man. Wray had saved his life, but that only meant that the puncher did not like unfair odds. Travis went on carefully. "I was just trying to get an idea of what this country was like. I've heard there's been some trouble with rustling around here."

Wray nodded. "I figure those hombres who jumped you were cattle-lifters themselves. You must've interrupted them while they were trying to rustle a few head."

Travis did not tell him that the attack had come out of nowhere and was probably motivated by his investigation into Mayor Yates's murder. It might be better for now to let Wray think whatever he wanted to.

"You sound like you've been losing some stock on the Trident," Travis said as he spurred his horse into a walk alongside Wray. The two men were riding in the same direction Travis had been going before he was attacked.

"We've lost enough," Wray said grimly. "Maybe not as much as some of the other spreads hereabouts, but there's been enough rustling to make all of us edgy."

The marshal nodded. Part of his job was being a good judge of character, and Wray struck him as an honest young man, even if he was riding for McCabe. Travis decided to tell him some of the truth. "That's why I came out here today," he said. "I want to find out who's behind this rustling."

Wray glanced over at him. "You some kind of range detective?"

Montgomery Stubb had asked him the same question the night before, and then Travis denied it. Now he said vaguely, "Something like that."

Wray laughed shortly. "I can tell you who's running that gang of crooks, if that's what you want to know. It's a fella called Lawton, Doak Lawton."

Travis had not heard of Doak Lawton and said as much. "What makes you think this Lawton is behind the rustling?" he asked.

Wray shrugged. "Lawton's a hardcase," he said. "Folks have suspected he was mixed up with everything that's shady around here for a long time. Sheriff Dehner can't seem to get any evidence against him, though. So Lawton and his bunch keep getting away with whatever they're doing."

"Lawton has his own gang, does he?"

Wray nodded. "They're about the roughest collection of men you'll find. Wouldn't surprise me if those four who ran you to ground were part of his bunch." The young cowboy reined in and leaned forward in his saddle. Travis brought his own horse to a stop as Wray frowned at him and went on. "You're asking a lot of questions, Mr. Travis. I think before I answer any more you'd better tell me what you're really after."

Travis hesitated for a moment, then met Wray's level stare with one of his own. "Do you know who Ruth Carson is?"

"Sure." Wray nodded. "She's that newspaper lady from Cheyenne who killed the mayor. They're going to hang her in a few days, aren't they?"

"Not if I can help it," Travis replied grimly. "I'm her brother-in-law, and I'm also the marshal of Abilene, Kansas. I've come to Wyoming to prove that Ruth is innocent. I intend to see that the real killer is caught."

Wray's eyes widened in surprise. "The jury found the Carson woman guilty," he said.

"I know, but she didn't do it."

"Then who did?"

Travis looked at the young man and said, "If I'm right, it was your boss—Flint McCabe."

Chapter Eight

————◆————

JOEL WRAY, HIS EYES HOODED AND THOUGHTFUL, stared at Luke Travis for a long moment. Finally he said, "Mayor Yates and Mr. McCabe were partners. I guess that's enough to make anybody think McCabe might have had something to do with the murder. But I don't see that McCabe came out ahead by the mayor's dying. Penny Yates inherited her daddy's share."

"I met the young lady yesterday," Travis told him. "She's not going to cross McCabe in anything that he wants to do. Besides, McCabe intends to marry her. If he does, he'll have the whole shooting match right in his pocket."

Wray considered that, and Travis saw embers beginning to smolder in the young cowhand's eyes as he did so. "You could be right," Wray said at last. "I've been riding for Trident long enough to know that Mr.

McCabe does what he wants to most of the time. Thinks he's going to marry Miss Yates, does he?"

"That's what he said yesterday when I ran into him at her house."

Wray grunted. Then he turned to the marshal with a puzzled expression. "If you're trying to find out who killed the mayor, why all the questions about the rustling around here?"

"I've got a hunch it's all tied together somehow," Travis replied. "I can't tell you why, Wray, but I think it would be worthwhile to find out who's behind all the thieving."

"I told you that. Doak Lawton's the man."

Travis shrugged. "Could be. You know the man, and I don't. Does he strike you as the sort who could be the brains behind a big rustling operation?"

Wray thought about that for a moment, then laughed. "Like I said, Lawton's a hardcase, but I'm not sure he's smart enough to set up a deal like that. You think that McCabe's mixed up in the cow-lifting?"

Travis hesitated. He did not know how long Wray had been riding for McCabe, or what the cowboy might have done in the past. He said carefully, "I've heard that the Trident herds had a pretty sudden growing spell a few years back."

"I wouldn't know," Wray replied. "I've only been in these parts for a little over a year. Trident was a big spread when I drifted up from Texas and signed on."

Travis nodded. That would explain why Wray seemed to be a little more objective about the situation than Travis had expected at first. Naturally, the young puncher had some loyalty to the brand he rode for, but he was not a long-term McCabe follower.

"Do you have any idea where I could find Lawton?" Travis asked.

"He and his men hang out at a roadhouse north of here," Wray replied. "I could take you there, but I'm supposed to be checking this range for stray steers."

"Wouldn't want you to get into any trouble. If you'll just tell me where to find the place, I'll ride up there, see what I can find out."

Wray's tanned face broke into a grin. "You're going into that outlaw's den by yourself, Marshal?"

Travis smiled at the young cowhand. "I don't plan to tell anybody I'm a lawman," he said dryly. "I just want to ask a few questions."

"Men in places like that don't usually take kindly to questions from a stranger—or even from somebody who's not. Tell you what, I'll ride with you."

"I thought you had work to do here."

Wray's grin widened. "I don't want to miss the fireworks when you ride into Cue Ball."

"That's what they call the place?"

"Yep." Wray nodded. "It's got the only billiard table between Cheyenne and Casper."

"Maybe we can get a game in," Travis said.

Wray laughed, and the two men continued riding north.

As he rode, Travis realized what a stroke of luck it had been that he had encountered Joel Wray. Wray had undoubtedly saved his life when he was pinned down, and now it appeared that the young man might be a good source of information about what was going on in the area. Travis had already learned more from him than he had in several hours of pumping people in Cheyenne.

They rode in companionable silence for a few

minutes, then Travis asked, "What led you to come up to Wyoming, anyway?"

Wray chuckled. "If you're asking whether I was on the run from the Texas law, Marshal, then the answer is no. I guess I was just a little restless. I'd been on a cattle drive up to the Montana boomtowns a couple of years ago, and we passed through this country along the way. I liked the looks of it and decided to come back. Didn't have anything to keep me in Texas. My folks are both dead, the rest of my kin scattered here and there." The young man shrugged. "Like I said, I drifted."

"How do you like working for McCabe?"

Wray took his time answering, obviously turning the question over in his mind. "It hasn't been bad," he finally said. "Trident pays about the same as the other spreads, and the cook sets a good table. The crew's not the friendliest I ever worked with, but we get along all right most of the time." He snorted. "There are a few boys who think they're mighty fast with a gun, but I just try to stay out of their way."

"Pistoleros, eh?" Travis said.

"Or what passes for it up here. Down home, they'd still be fast, but nothing that special."

Travis glanced away so that Wray would not see the grin on his face. Like most of the Texans Travis had met, Wray seemed to think that folks from the Lone Star State were naturally bigger, faster, and tougher.

"How often did Yates come out to the ranch?" he asked a moment later. "It was half his, after all."

"Maybe so, but McCabe made sure everybody knew *he* gave the orders on the Trident, not Yates. The mayor didn't seem to mind. From what I saw he was more comfortable in town. But he did ride out to the ranch house sometimes, to talk things over with McCabe, I guess." Wray's voice softened. "Miss Penny came with him every now and then, too. We all looked forward to that."

Travis glanced over and saw the expression on Wray's face. The young man was obviously thinking about Penny Yates, and Travis guessed that he cared a great deal for her. Of course, any cowboy stuck out on the range for days and weeks at a time would welcome the sight of a pretty female face, but Wray's reaction seemed different from that of the usual lovesick puncher. There was something honest about it, something that went beyond simple physical attraction.

Could Wray be in love with Penny Yates? Travis wondered. "Did you ever show her around the ranch?" he asked.

The sudden flush on Wray's face told Travis his guess had hit home. "I don't reckon that's any of your business, Marshal," Wray snapped.

"Sorry," Travis murmured, and then fell silent as he mulled over what Wray had told him so far. He was not going to push the matter, but Wray was wrong about one thing—Travis was making everything that had gone on in Cheyenne and on the Trident range his business until he had sorted out Yates's murder.

Wray set their course, angling a little east of north to strike the trail between Cheyenne and Casper. After they had ridden for a while in silence, Travis asked, "Are we still on Trident range?"

Wray nodded. "Yes. We have to cross two more creeks before we come to the boundary. McCabe's bought a lot of land up this way. He keeps expanding the spread."

That was interesting, Travis thought. Clearly,

McCabe was not hurting for money. Yates's death had not disrupted the day-to-day operation of the ranch or interfered with McCabe's plans for expansion.

He suddenly wondered if McCabe had been building up the ranch at the expense of the partners' other holdings. That might not have sat well with Yates, might have even led to a quarrel between the two men.

If only the case against Ruth had not been so cut-and-dried, Travis thought, Flint McCabe surely would have emerged as the leading suspect in Yates's death. The manner of the mayor's death had certainly been convenient for McCabe.

The two men rode on, their conversation sporadic as they eventually left the Trident ranch behind. Wray pointed out the creek that formed the northern boundary of the ranch as they forded the small stream. The terrain here was rolling prairie with, as always, the foothills and the mountains looming to the west.

It was well past noon, and Travis's stomach growled as a reminder. "Do you think we can get something to eat at that roadhouse?" he asked as they rode up a small rise.

When he reached the top, Wray pulled his horse to a stop and nodded at the building in the broad, shallow valley below. "I reckon we'll find out soon enough," he said with a grin. "There's Cue Ball."

Travis reined in beside Wray and studied the landscape. A large two-story building with smoke curling from the chimney stood in the center of the valley. A couple of one-room shacks huddled near the roadhouse, and farther down the valley a church roof and steeple reached for the sky from a stand of trees.

"Sort of a strange place for a church," Travis commented.

"Not really," Wray replied. "Folks can do their celebrating at Cue Ball, then ride down the road and say a prayer when they sober up. Probably works out pretty well."

Travis grinned. "The way you make this place sound, if we get out alive we'd better go put something in the poor box."

"Might be a good idea," Wray said, and Travis could not be sure if the cowboy was serious or not.

Wray started down the hill, and Travis rode alongside him. The marshal could see the wagon road approaching Cue Ball from the south and then winding on north toward Casper. It looked like a well-traveled route. A wagon and a dozen horses were tied up in front of the roadhouse. The place appeared to be busy this afternoon.

"There's no guarantee Lawton will be here," Wray said in a low voice as he and Travis approached the building. "But with that many horses out front, there's a good chance he is."

Travis nodded. They pulled up and found places for their horses at the crowded hitch rail. As they stepped onto the porch, Travis realized he should have gone to see Ruth before leaving Cheyenne that morning. If he did not make it out of here alive, chances were she would never learn what had happened to him. Not that she would have long to worry about it if he failed, he thought grimly.

The roadhouse called Cue Ball was built of broad, weathered planks and had only a few windows and two doors, one at each end of the building. No sign on the place announced its name, but Travis was sure that everyone in this part of the country knew about it.

Wray and he stepped into the dimly lit building. The windows were so grimy that much of the sunlight was cut out. A couple of lanterns gave off a feeble glow.

Travis paused and scanned the interior. A wall divided the place roughly in half. Wray and he had entered on the side that served as a saloon, with a bar on one wall and a few tables scattered around the room. A steep staircase at the end of the bar led to a balcony with second-floor rooms opening off it.

Through an open door in the dividing partition, Travis could see that the other half of the building was used as a general store. Barrels of flour, crackers, sugar, and pickles stood in a row on the floor. Bolts of cloth were stacked on tables. Harnesses and farm implements hung from hooks on the walls. A settler, his wife, and four children were rummaging through the goods, and Travis surmised they had come in the wagon tied up outside. Immigrants passing through, he thought, who would probably be all right as long as they stayed where they were and did not venture into this half of the roadhouse.

The billiard table that gave the place its name sat in the center of the room. Several men stood around it watching as two players awkwardly hit the balls around the table. More customers were sitting at the tables, and a couple of men lounged at the bar with mugs of beer in their hands. All the men wore dusty clothes and tied-down guns. Travis could tell that they were all hardcases, men who had no respect for law and order and little for plain common decency. The only woman in sight was the immigrant's wife in the next room.

As Travis and Wray came in, the Cue Ball's patrons briefly studied the newcomers with cold-eyed stares. Then the two carrying billiard cues went back to their game, and the spectators turned their attention back to the table. The others began to drink again. The only person who continued to watch Travis and Wray was one of the pair standing at the bar. He did not take his eyes off them as they approached.

Wray stepped up to the bar and said to the thin, jug-eared bartender, "I'll take a beer, Smitty, and so will my friend here."

The bartender bobbed his head and started to draw the beers. Travis stopped beside Wray, met the gaze of the man who was watching them, and nodded. "Howdy," he said.

The man nodded in return. He was a little shorter than Travis, but heavier, with wide, powerful shoulders. He wore brown whipcord pants, a dingy shirt that had once been white, and a black vest. His black hat had a tightly rolled brim, the front of which curved over dark eyes with bushy brows. A heavy black mustache drooped over his mouth, and the skin of his lean cheeks was pocked. Even without seeing the well-worn grips of the pistol on the man's hip, Travis would have known him for a bad one.

Wray sipped the beer that the bartender shoved in front of him, then asked, "How are you, Lawton?"

"Tolerable," the dark-eyed man answered in a growling voice. "What the hell are you doin' up here, Wray? Get lost chasin' one of your boss's cows?"

"Just rode up for a drink."

Lawton switched his gaze back to Travis, who was

sampling his own warm, flat beer. "How about you, mister?"

Travis's voice was as hard as Lawton's as he replied, "Can't a man get a drink without being bothered with a bunch of questions?"

"We don't see too many strangers around here. Can't blame a man for being curious." Lawton thumped his mug on the bar and edged a little closer to Travis. "You plan on answerin' or not?"

"Take it easy, Lawton," Wray said sharply. "We don't want trouble."

"That's right," Travis added. He had come here for information, not a brawl. He went on. "No offense meant, mister. I just came up from Kansas looking for a little work. Ran into Wray here, and he offered to buy me a drink. We knew each other back in Abilene."

Travis was doing some guessing, but from the things Wray had said, he thought it was likely the young man had been part of the many cattle drives from Texas to the railheads in Kansas. It was feasible they could have met there. The story would do for Lawton's benefit, anyway.

"You don't look much like a cowhand," Lawton said, glancing at Travis's hands and clothes and gun.

Travis shook his head. "I'm not," he said simply.

"Looking for gun work, are you?" Lawton asked bluntly.

Travis was equally direct. "Could be. You know where a man could find some?"

Lawton did not answer for a long moment as he studied Travis. Finally, he said, "I can always use another good man." He glanced at Wray. "Cowboy, why don't you finish your drink and get out of here?"

Clearly, he did not want to discuss business with Wray around, which was another point in the young man's favor as far as Travis was concerned. Wray was probably honest if a man like Lawton did not trust him.

Travis gave a minuscule nod as Wray darted a look at him. He drained half of his beer and then said, "Sure, if that's what Travis wants. It's none of my business what you boys talk about."

"You're pretty smart for a cowhand, Wray," Lawton said coolly. "Stay that way."

Wray grunted and lifted his beer to finish it. Travis waited patiently. Lawton had sized him up and evidently been impressed with what he had seen. Travis was certainly willing to talk to him about possibly joining the gang. That would be the quickest way to find out what Lawton was up to.

Lawton had impressed him as a dangerous man, a man not to be crossed. It was easy to believe that he was part of the rustling ring that was plaguing the territory, but it also struck Travis as unlikely that he was the man behind the operation. Lawton could handle the actual rustling and deal with any opposition his men and he ran into, but someone else was planning it, Travis speculated.

Wray thumped his empty mug on the bar, shot Travis one last look, and turned to leave the roadhouse. Travis had a feeling that the young man would stay close at hand, though.

Wray did not reach the door. "Say, can a man get a drink in here?" a new voice asked from the doorway between the saloon and the general store.

Everyone in the room turned. The man who had

stopped for supplies with his family was standing there with a cocky grin on his face. Worse yet, Travis saw, he was wearing a new-looking Smith & Wesson revolver in a holster that was belted high around his waist. On his feet were shoes instead of boots, and his clothes would have been more at home in a town than in this roadhouse in the middle of rugged Wyoming Territory. He was a greenhorn, pure and simple, and Travis knew the man was trouble as soon as he saw him swagger into the saloon.

The men standing around the billiard table laughed. "What the hell've we got here?" one of them asked. "I never seen nothin' like it before."

"That's because you ain't never been back east, Ben," another man said. "Hell, they got piss-ants like this one scurryin' all over them cities."

The greenhorn paused as if suddenly realizing that he was about to get into a situation he could not handle. Watching from the bar, Travis hoped that he had the sense to back through the door, rejoin his family, and get out of Cue Ball while he still could. But then stubborn pride flashed in the man's eyes, and he forged ahead, striding past the billiard table and heading for the bar.

One of the billiard players casually thrust his cue between the man's legs. His calves banged painfully against it, and his balance deserted him. He waved his arms for an instant in an attempt to regain his footing, then fell heavily on the floor.

"William!" the man's wife called in alarm from the doorway. Travis looked over and saw her standing there, her hands lifted to her face, her features twisted in a worried expression. She had probably tried to talk her husband out of stepping into the saloon for a drink, Travis thought, but his pride had sent him anyway. The same pride that had just caused him to fall on his face.

Coming to the door was the worst thing the woman could have done. The hardcases had been willing to ignore her as long as she stayed in the store, but now that she had ventured into their territory, she was fair game. Travis saw she was not particularly attractive, but that would not mean much to men like these.

One of them let out a whoop and said to the greenhorn, "Looks like your woman's goin' to come protect you, Will-yum."

The easterner scrambled to his feet. "You leave her out of this!" he said hotly. "All I wanted was a drink, and you men had no right to assault me."

"Talks fancy, don't he?" another of Lawton's men asked. "What do you say, boys? Should we teach him a lesson, or do you reckon we should just dance a little with his wife instead?"

"I'm for dancin'," one man said with a leer. "An' anything else that gal wants to do!"

The woman paled and started backing out of the doorway. Her husband's reaction was just the opposite. His face flushed angrily, and he stepped forward. "I said to leave her alone!" he snapped.

A man reached out, put a hand on his shoulder, and shoved, sending him sprawling against one of the tables. At the same time, another hardcase quickly stepped toward the woman, grasped her arm, and pulled her into the room. She cried out in fear and pain.

Travis glanced at Lawton. As he watched his men

have their fun with the immigrant couple, his face was expressionless, but his dark eyes glinted in amusement. Obviously he would not do anything to stop what was happening.

Joel Wray softly muttered a curse, and the young cowboy's features were tight with anger. Travis could see that Wray wanted to step in and put a stop to the abuse.

So did Travis. All of his instincts told him that the greenhorn was liable to get hurt. But if he got mixed up in this, his budding relationship with Doak Lawton would probably be wrecked.

The easterner staggered against the table and caught himself. As he straightened, his hand went toward the gun on his hip. He was slow and awkward, and several of Lawton's men reached for their own weapons, their eyes gleaming at the chance for a killing.

Travis had to act. He palmed out his Colt with deceptive speed and brought the barrel up as he eared back the hammer. While the click of the gun cocking seemed louder than it really was, it was plainly audible over the woman's frightened sobs.

"You boys hold still," Travis growled at Lawton's men. "Let's leave the guns out of this."

None of them had drawn their weapons before Travis's action had caused them to freeze. They stayed that way, knowing full well that he had the drop on them, but they looked at Lawton to see what he wanted them to do.

Wray had his hand on the butt of his pistol, and he was equally watchful. It was clear he was impressed by the speed of Travis's draw.

Lawton was still lounging at the bar. A faint smile curved his lips under the heavy mustache. "Don't reckon that's a smart thing to do, buttin' in on my boys' fun like that."

"I just don't want to see anybody get hurt," Travis said evenly. He looked at the easterner, who was standing as motionless as his tormentors. "Mister, you'd best get your wife and kids and get out of here while you can."

"But—"

"Do it!" Travis's voice crackled with command, cutting off any protest the man was about to make.

He swallowed nervously, nodded, and hurried over to his wife. The man who had been holding her arm released her. Her husband slipped an arm around her shoulders and hustled her out of the saloon. Travis heard him calling urgently to his children to come with him.

A moment later he heard the slam of the other door, and then, a few seconds after that, the creak of wheels as the wagon pulled away from the building. The cries of the easterner as he whipped up his team carried back into the roadhouse.

"All right, they're gone," Lawton said. "What now?"

"Well . . . I hope we can go back to having that drink and talking about business."

Lawton shook his head. "I don't reckon the boys would want to work with you now, mister. And like the old sayin' goes, if you ain't with us, you're agin us. You made a mistake comin' here."

"Maybe," Travis agreed grimly. "I think I'll just ride out, then."

Wray spoke up. "And I'll back his play, Lawton." The cowboy had slipped his gun from its holster.

Lawton glanced at him. "You're makin' a worse

mistake than this bastard, Wray. I ain't holdin' nothin' against you. You can still walk out of here if you want to."

Wray shook his head and said, "I'll stay."

"Suit yourself," Lawton said, shrugging his heavy shoulders. He flicked a nod at the bartender.

The jug-eared man behind the bar suddenly whipped up the bottle in front of him and flung it at Wray. His aim was good. The heavy glass bottle smacked into Wray's arm, knocking it aside. The gun in his hand blasted, but the bullet thudded harmlessly into the wall of the roadhouse.

At the same instant, Lawton dashed his beer into Travis's face. Then he bellowed and charged, sweeping aside the marshal's gun arm as he bowled into him.

Travis was driven back against the bar. As he slammed against the hardwood he grunted in pain. He chopped at Lawton's head with his pistol, but the hardcase's hat absorbed most of the blow's force. Over Lawton's shoulder, Travis saw the other men closing in on them.

He triggered twice, sending the slugs over the heads of Lawton's men. The shots were enough to slow them down. Lawton pounded hammerlike punches into Travis's middle while he held him pinned against the bar. Travis got his free hand on Lawton's jaw and shoved as hard as he could.

Lawton fell back slightly. Travis drove an elbow into his face, making him give a little more ground. He slashed at Lawton's head with the gun again.

This time the blow landed heavily. Lawton staggered. At that moment, the bartender looped an arm around Travis's neck and pulled him halfway up onto the bar. Travis gasped for breath but lifted his leg and planted a booted foot in Lawton's midsection. He straightened the leg and viciously shoved Lawton into the midst of his men. Several of them went sprawling along with Lawton.

Wray appeared at Travis's side, snatched a whiskey bottle that was on the bar, and clouted the bartender over the head with it. The man released his grip around Travis's neck, and the marshal slid back onto his feet and began gasping for breath.

He did not have much time to recover before two of Lawton's men swarmed over him. He blocked their blows as best he could and threw some punches of his own. Beside him, Wray was doing the same thing, holding his own as he battled the angry men.

But Travis knew it was only a matter of time before they were overwhelmed. Once that happened, Lawton's men would probably stomp them to death.

He ducked under a roundhouse punch and suddenly threw himself forward, knocking one of the men aside. Travis went down, rolled, and came up next to the billiard table. He reached out and plucked up one of the cue sticks. Jamming his gun back in its holster, he charged, whipping the cue around his head wickedly.

Lawton's men fell back, but two of them did not get out of the way in time. The stick cracked across the face of one, pulping his nose, then shattered on the skull of the second, knocking him out of the fight. Travis's charge brought him to Wray's side. He caught the young cowboy's arm and propelled him toward the door.

"Run for it!" Travis rasped. He dropped the splintered cue stick, drew his gun, and fired three times as he ran toward the door behind Wray. These were not warning shots. One bullet shattered the shoulder of a man who had drawn his gun. Another punched through a thigh and dropped a second man. The final bullet burned a furrow along the forearm of yet another of Lawton's men and forced him to drop his gun. By the time the last shot had been fired, Travis was diving through the door behind Wray.

The cowhand vaulted onto his horse and leaned over to jerk loose the reins of Travis's mare. Grabbing the saddle horn, Travis mounted in a flash. He wheeled his horse and banged his heels against its flanks, urging it into a gallop beside Wray's horse. Side by side, the two men pounded away from the roadhouse.

Travis glanced over his shoulder and then called into the wind buffeting his face, "Doesn't look like they're coming after us!"

Wray looked back and nodded in agreement. "We put up too much of a fight," he called over the thunder of hoofbeats. "And Lawton was out cold!"

The two men rode hard for several miles, but when there was still no sign of pursuit, they pulled up and let their winded horses walk for a while. "Are you all right?" Travis asked the cowhand.

"Sure." Wray rubbed his arm. "I'll be a little sore where that bottle hit me, and there'll probably be a few more bruises, but nothing that won't heal. I'm just sorry you didn't get to talk to Lawton more before that fight started. You didn't learn much."

Travis shrugged. He shared Wray's disappointment, but he tried to look at it positively. "At least I got to meet Lawton," he said. "He seems like the type that might be mixed up in rustling, all right, but I don't think he's running the ring. Maybe I would have gotten closer to the ringleader if things had happened differently; maybe I wouldn't." He laughed shortly and humorlessly. "But at least we stirred things up a little. Sometimes that can get results by itself."

Wray laughed, too, and then lifted a hand to check his mouth. When he drew his fingers away, they had blood on them. "I'd say we stirred things up a lot," he said dryly.

Chapter Nine

FOR THE FIRST TIME IN HIS PROFESSIONAL CAREER PHINEAS Kingsley Nelson was having doubts about what he was supposed to do.

This was unique, because he had a deep respect for the law and believed in the rightness of what he was doing. He had been a hangman for ten years, traveling all over the frontier from Texas to Missouri to Montana. Most of the time he moved from town to town in response to summonses from judges and lawmen to do his grim work. Occasionally he would stay in one area and work on a regular basis for a local judge. Over the years his reputation had grown, largely because he had hanged some of the most notorious outlaws in the West.

Nelson looked upon his occupation as a science and took great pride in his professionalism. Throwing a rope over a tree limb and hoisting a man up to dangle helplessly until he strangled was barbaric in his eyes.

His trapdoors worked smoothly and cleanly. The rope was always the correct length, the knot just right, and the fall was perfectly timed. The neck of the person being executed had always broken just as it was supposed to.

But the necks of those hardcases and killers had never been as smooth and soft as Ruth Carson's.

As he went about supervising the construction of the gallows, he found he could not keep the image of her face out of his mind. It was his practice to oversee the work, but this time he was doing it automatically, without really thinking or seeing the scaffold take shape. Instead, he recalled her angry expression and flashing brown eyes when she practically threw him out of the jail.

At that moment Ruth Carson appeared to be in charge, not Sheriff Will Dehner. She obviously had the kind of forceful personality that made such things possible. Nelson could understand why she had been able to make a success of her newspaper.

He could also imagine her taking a strong stand against anyone with whom she disagreed—like Mayor Roland T. Yates. But for her to have killed the man, poisoned him as if he were vermin . . . Nelson could not believe that, not after meeting her.

However, the evidence against her had been strong enough for a jury to convict her. In the past a jury's conviction had been sufficient for P. K. Nelson. He never lost a minute's sleep over the men he executed because he was fully confident of their guilt.

It was different with Ruth.

By late in the afternoon the main frame of the scaffold had been erected and only a little work remained. Nelson told the men working for him that they could stop for the day. Local men hired by Sheriff Dehner, his crew were more than happy to stop work. It would only take a few hours the next morning to install the trapdoor and the lever-and-bar mechanism that would release the door at the proper moment. Then the gallows would be complete and ready for testing. After that the structure would stand waiting for a day, as a grim reminder of what was going to happen at nine o'clock on Friday morning.

In the fading light Nelson examined the workmanship. He checked the height of the platform and the beam suspended above it. Everything looked correct, just like the plans he had drawn after meeting Ruth Carson. He was confident that it would work perfectly when the time came.

Heaving a sigh and shaking his head, he walked away from the gallows and did not look back. He felt his features settling into a dour expression that was so different from the jolly one he usually wore. Normally during the construction of a gallows, he had his crew laughing all day at the jokes and yarns that he spun so naturally. But today had been different. The work had proceeded in a somber atmosphere. Under the circumstances, most people would expect that, but it bothered Nelson.

He had to know the truth, he decided as he walked past the courthouse. He had to be convinced to his own satisfaction that he was doing the right thing. And the only way to do that was to talk to Ruth Carson again. He turned toward the sheriff's office.

When Nelson arrived at the office, a young deputy

wearing spectacles was sitting behind the sheriff's scarred desk. Nelson smiled as he stepped inside and met the young man's quizzical gaze. "Hello, son," he said heartily, his voice taking on some of its usual jolly, booming tone. "Is Sheriff Dehner around?"

The deputy shook his head. "He's down at the café. Can I help you?" Before Nelson could reply, the young man's eyes lit up. "Say, I know who you are!" he exclaimed. "You're the hangman."

"That's right, son. P. K. Nelson, at your service. I was wondering if I could ask a favor of you."

"Why, sure, Mr. Nelson. What can I do for you?"

Nelson nodded toward the cellblock door. "I'd like to talk to your prisoner for a few minutes, alone if possible."

The deputy pursed his lips and looked uncertain. "I don't know," he said slowly. "I'm not sure how the sheriff would feel about it."

At that moment, the door opened, and a stout middle-aged woman bustled into the office, carrying a cloth-covered tray. "Hello, Jeremy," she said brightly. "The sheriff sent me over with Miss Carson's supper—" She abruptly stopped speaking when she noticed that there was someone else in the office.

Nelson whirled around and reached out toward the woman. "Here, ma'am, let me take that for you," he said with a charming smile. He inhaled deeply. "Umm, smells delicious!"

The woman flushed with pleasure. "Why, thank you, sir."

"Yes, ma'am," Nelson went on quickly as he circled the desk with the tray, "if there's one thing I know, it's good food. Why, I'd be willing to wager that this is some of the best in Cheyenne. No, in the whole territory." As he spoke he plucked the ring of keys from the nail on the wall.

"Wait a minute, Mr. Nelson," the deputy said, scraping back his chair and standing hurriedly. "You can't—"

His protest came too late. Nelson had already unlocked the door and was swinging it open. The hangman glanced over his shoulder and said airily, "Don't worry, Jeremy. We're on the same side, after all."

Jeremy did not look convinced, but he said no more and frowned at Nelson nervously. As Nelson turned, he heard the young deputy tell the woman that he would return the tray later.

Inside the cellblock, Nelson paused in front of the door and watched Ruth Carson rise from the rocking chair with a surprised look on her face. "Why, Mr. Nelson! What are you doing back here?"

"Just bringing you your supper, Miss Carson," he replied, smiling as pleasantly as he could at her.

She met his gaze coolly. "I seem to recall telling you this morning that I had nothing to say to you. Now that I remember why your name was familiar to me, I should think it would be obvious how I feel."

Nelson's smile slipped slightly. "Oh. So you know who I am."

"I'm a journalist, Mr. Nelson," Ruth replied acidly, *"not* a blithering idiot—although some people would say those things are one and the same. I've run across your name in stories about the fates of outlaws and . . . murderers."

Nelson hesitated. She was just as lovely as he remembered, and the anger sparking in her brown eyes this evening only made her more attractive. "At least let me give you this tray," he said. "Then, if you don't want to talk to me, I'll leave without complaint."

Ruth moved over to the bars and took the tray that he passed through the special opening in the door. She started to say something, paused thoughtfully, and then asked, "Why do you insist upon talking to me, Mr. Nelson? I can't imagine you're this interested in all your victims."

He winced. "I prefer not to think of them that way, ma'am. They were criminals, every single one of them. Innocent people were their victims, not the other way around."

"I'm a criminal, at least according to the judge and jury," Ruth said bitterly.

Nelson took a deep breath and shot a glance at the closed door that led to the sheriff's office. In a low voice, he said, "Yes, but I'm not at all sure you're guilty."

For a moment Ruth was speechless. She stared at him in surprise, then very deliberately turned and placed the supper tray on her bed. Slowly returning to the bars, she asked, "What did you say?"

"I said I'm not sure you did what they say you did," Nelson replied. "For some reason I can't believe that a lady like you would . . . would kill anyone."

Ruth said nothing for almost a full minute. The long, uncanny silence made Nelson uneasy, but he was even more uncomfortable under the penetrating gaze she fixed on him. He tried to meet her eyes squarely as she searched his face.

Finally she said quietly, "I think I believe you, Mr. Nelson. I'm not sure how you reached your conclusion—"

"Neither am I, dear lady," he cut in earnestly.

"—but you are correct. I didn't kill anyone. I wouldn't kill anyone, not unless it was to save someone else's life. I'm not sure I could do it even then."

"But all the evidence at the trial . . . ?"

"Was certainly damning, but entirely circumstantial," Ruth insisted. "If you're interested, you can go over to my newspaper office and read a complete account of the trial in our back numbers." She smiled. "I've read my associate's stories in the paper. They're quite accurate."

"I'm sure they are," Nelson muttered. His frown deepened. This visit to the jail, rather than reassuring him that he would be doing the right thing by carrying out the sentence of the court, had only increased his doubts.

He had questioned Ruth Carson's guilt. Now he was certain that she was innocent. What could he do about it?

She must have sensed his distress, because she said sincerely, "I'm sorry if this makes it more difficult for you, Mr. Nelson. I'm a law-abiding woman, and I will go to the gallows as the court has decreed. But I will go protesting my innocence every step of the way."

Nelson had trouble finding his voice. After a few seconds, he said, "Of course." Then a thought occurred to him. "But perhaps something will happen. I know that your brother-in-law is in town. He struck me as a very competent man. Maybe he can discover some new evidence—"

"I'm praying for that," Ruth said. "But I don't have a great deal of hope, Mr. Nelson." She chuckled dryly. "I'm afraid that miracles happen only rarely."

Nelson took a deep breath, then gestured at the tray

on the bed. "You'd best eat your supper while it's still hot, Miss Carson. You need to keep your strength up. You never know what will happen between now and Friday morning."

With that, he nodded, turned, and walked out of the cellblock. The young deputy looked suspiciously at him as he reentered the office. "What was that about?" he demanded.

"You didn't eavesdrop, did you?"

Jeremy flushed. "Of course not. A prisoner's got a right to have visitors, and I don't reckon a man like you would do anything stupid, like try to pass her a gun."

"Let me give you a little advice, son. Never think you've got a man completely figured out. Soon as you do, he'll come up with something to surprise you."

"You *didn't* give her a gun, did you?"

Nelson laughed. "No, of course not. I just had some personal business to discuss with the lady."

"Do I tell Sheriff Dehner that you came by and talked to Miss Carson?"

"No reason not to. I don't have any secrets from the sheriff."

At least not yet, Nelson thought. But he had made a decision, a decision with which he had had to struggle. This visit to Ruth had been the last factor in determining his course of action.

Luke Travis was not the only one who could investigate this case, Nelson thought as he left the sheriff's office. For the first time in his career, he was going to poke around in a criminal matter himself. If any evidence had been overlooked, P. K. Nelson was going to find it.

* * *

Penny Yates felt very alone these days, even though a cook and an Irish maid lived in the house with her, and an old man, who served as handyman and carriage driver, stayed in rooms above the carriage house. Ever since her father died, things had not been right. The grief was still fresh, of course; she did not expect to be over that for quite a while. But the loneliness of her life surprised her.

It was strange, she thought. Her father had not spent much time at home when he was alive. The business of running the town, along with managing the holdings that he and Flint McCabe had accumulated, kept Mayor Yates away from his house most of the time. Penny was lucky to share two or three meals a week with him.

But that time together, limited though it was, meant more to her than her father probably knew, more than she herself was aware of. She had not realized how much she would miss him until he was gone.

But there was no turning back the clock. He was gone, and she had to look to the future. Even if that future included Flint McCabe.

She only wished that her feelings toward him were the same as his were for her. He had watched her grow from an awkward child into a woman, and sometime during those years, he had begun to look differently at her. No longer was he content to be Uncle Flint, her friend and occasional confidant, the man who had taught her how to ride a horse.

He wanted to marry her. And Penny saw no other way that her own future would be secure.

But she was in love with another man, and there was no getting around that fact. . . .

She had picked at her supper, finding the well-prepared meal tasteless as she had found everything since her father died, before retiring to the parlor to try to read. It was difficult to concentrate on the words. She kept thinking about her father's death and Ruth Carson and that man Travis, who had come to see her the day before. She had never doubted that Ruth was guilty. She knew how much trouble the woman had given her father. Every time there had been an unfavorable editorial about the mayor in the *Cheyenne Eagle,* all of Penny's protective instincts surged to the fore. Her mother had died when Penny was barely out of her childhood, and since that time she had been taking care of her father. Naturally, he thought it was the other way around. But when he really needed her, she was not there. He died on the side of the road by himself.

Now Luke Travis was in Cheyenne to open wounds, to cast doubts so that justice might not be done. Anger flared inside Penny as she thought about it.

A knock on the front door made her glance up impatiently from her book. She usually answered the door herself, but tonight she did not want to bother with it. The knock was repeated, and a moment later she heard the maid leave the kitchen and move down the hall to the front door.

Penny listened to the murmuring voices and realized that the visitor was a man. She did not recognize his voice, and she tried to force her attention back to the pages of the book in front of her. Unless the visitor was someone important, Penny was confident the maid would send him away.

"Miss Penny, I think ye'd better be seein' this lad. He insists he has somethin' that belongs to ye."

Penny looked up at the maid standing in the doorway of the parlor. She closed her book with an exasperated thump. "Very well," she snapped impatiently, "but this had better be important." She rose and stepped toward the doorway as the maid backed away to allow the visitor to enter the parlor.

When she saw who it was, Penny stopped in her tracks, dumbfounded. Simon Smith took a step into the parlor, then halted and glanced nervously around him. His arms were pressed tightly to his sides, and he kept his feet and legs together, holding himself in as if he were afraid he would break something in the room. Knowing how clumsy Simon could be, Penny would not have been surprised if that had happened.

In an attempt to hide her annoyance, she took a deep breath and then smiled. Snapping at Simon was useless. It would only hurt his feelings, and he would be even less communicative than ever. "What can I do for you, Simon?" she asked as pleasantly as she could.

He tentatively raised one arm and held out a thick sheaf of papers, bound together with string. As he thrust them toward her, he swallowed and said, "I think these are yours, Miss Penny."

Perplexed, Penny frowned. Like nearly everyone else in Cheyenne, she had known Simon for years. She knew that he sometimes got funny ideas, and when he did, it was hard to convince him of the truth. Rather than argue, it was usually easier just to agree with him.

Despite her determination to be pleasant, she found she was in no mood for him tonight. For one thing, Simon worked at the newspaper. Ruth Carson had taken him under her wing and tried to make a useful citizen out of him, a project that anyone in town could have told her was hopeless. Penny disliked him because he was associated with Ruth and also because he made her feel very strange when she passed him on the street. He was always unfailingly polite, but he was unreadable. There was no way to know what twisted thoughts crawled through his simple brain.

She stared at the papers in his hand but made no move to take them. "They're not mine," she said. "I've never seen them before. Where did you get them?"

"Found 'em at the newspaper office while I was cleanin' up," he replied. He insistently prodded the air with the papers. "They got your daddy's name on 'em."

Penny could think of several reasons why documents bearing her father's name would have been at the paper. "Perhaps it's a draft of an editorial or a news story someone wrote," she suggested impatiently.

Simon shook his head. "Nope. I've learned to read pretty good over to the school. Sometimes I go over at night, and the teacher helps me with my words. I think these papers was wrote by your daddy."

Penny reached out and snatched the sheaf from Simon's hand. "Give me those," she snapped. She undid the knot in the string tied around the papers and unfolded the bundle. If these were indeed her father's documents, then the newspaper had obtained them by illegal means.

Quickly she scanned the papers and saw that they were covered with writing scrawled in a familiar hand. It was her father's. Without looking further, she folded them up, wound the string around them, and began retying it.

"Thank you, Simon," she said stiffly. "These *did* belong to my father. I appreciate your bringing them to me." She repressed the urge to berate him. Ruth Carson was the one at fault, she told herself, not Simon. Ruth had stolen these documents somehow.

"It was no problem, Miss Penny. I don't like things clutterin' up all the nooks 'n crannies. Got to clean house ever' now 'n then."

He looked so solemn as he said it that Penny could not help but smile at him. "Well, thank you again," she said. He still stood there, not moving, until Penny said, "You can go now."

"Oh. Thanks, Miss Penny." He nodded and left. As she stared at the bundle in her hands, Penny vaguely heard the maid close the door behind Simon and scurry back to the kitchen. Frowning slightly, she carried the sheaf of papers to her father's desk, where a good-sized stack of documents was already piled on it. She decided she would add these to it. When she felt up to it, she would sit down with her father's lawyer and go through them. But that chore could wait until her mental state had improved.

She was about to lay the papers on the desk when something caught her eye. One of the sheets had become crooked while she was handling them, and part of it stuck out from the bundle so that she could read the writing on it. She noticed Flint McCabe's name entered there, and after it the sum $14,328.47.

It was entirely logical that McCabe's name would be on some of her father's records. After all, the two men had been partners. But if that sum represented a payment of some kind, it was a sizable one. Penny's curiosity was stirred, and without stopping to think about it, she slipped the string off the papers and spread them out on the desk.

She had never pretended to be interested in her father's business affairs and often listened to his discussions with half an ear. Nevertheless, she had spent several years at one of the finest schools for young ladies in St. Louis. She did not find it difficult to decipher the jumble of numbers and make sense of the records.

As she studied the documents, her frown deepened. If she was reading them correctly, they were a record of the profits realized by McCabe and her father's partnership. What made them unusual was that the numbers were much, much larger than Penny would have expected. A great deal of money had been flowing into the partnership; most of it came from something called the Great Plains Cattle Company in Laramie, Wyoming Territory.

Penny frequently overheard McCabe and her father discuss ranch business, but she could not recall ever hearing any mention of the cattle company in Laramie. Quite a few land transactions were also recorded in these papers, indicating that the partners had been steadily purchasing large tracts all over the territory. Penny had never heard anything about this, either.

An uneasy feeling stole over her, and she chewed her lip thoughtfully. Of course she was not privy to all the details of her father's business, nor had she been that interested, but something about these records made her nervous. Evidently there had been quite a bit that she had not known—until now.

She had every right to this information, she decided abruptly, but she wanted to examine it carefully first.

Instead of adding the papers to the others, she took a key from her pocket and unlocked the center drawer of the desk. She gathered the documents, tied the string around them, and slipped the bundle into the drawer. As she turned the key to lock it, she told herself that she would keep them to herself . . . until she had a chance to learn the truth.

Chapter Ten

———◆———

TRY AS SHE MIGHT, PENNY COULD NOT FORCE HER ATTEN-
tion back to the book she had been trying to read. It
was difficult before, but now, after seeing the mysterious documents written by her father, concentrating on
a novel became impossible.

She got up, went to the desk, and paused with
her hand resting on the center drawer for a moment. Then, sighing deeply, she made up her mind.
Unlocking the drawer, she took the papers out and
untied the string. As she unfolded the bundle and
began to study them again, a frown creased her fore-
head.

She examined them more thoroughly in this second
reading and found that the conclusions she had
reached in her first assessment were confirmed. The
partnership between Flint McCabe and her father had
been considerably more profitable than anyone real-

ized, and they had used those profits to expand their holdings at a dramatic rate.

If this kept up, Penny realized, McCabe and she would eventually own the whole territory. And if they were married, McCabe would control her share of the business as well.

The thought sent a chill up her spine. McCabe was well on his way to becoming the emperor of his own frontier kingdom. Would he have been willing to kill to have the prize all to himself?

A knock on the front door startled Penny from her reverie and made her gasp. The rapping was soft but insistent, and Penny recognized it with a surge of excitement. She hurriedly stuffed the papers into the desk and went to the door. It was now late enough that the maid would have retired for the night, and besides, Penny wanted to answer this summons herself.

She swung the door open and beamed a radiant smile at her visitor. He was a tall, handsome young man in dusty range clothes who held his hat in his hand.

Grinning rather sheepishly, Joel Wray said, "Good evening, Miss Penny. Sorry I didn't have time to get myself cleaned up. I've been riding most of the day. But I wanted to see you."

Penny moved back from the doorway to allow him to enter. "That's all right, Joel. Please, come in. Can I get you anything?"

"No, thanks, ma'am," he replied, shaking his head. As he stepped into the foyer, the spurs on his booted feet jingled softly and musically. "I hope it's not too late to come calling."

"Of course not. Won't you come into the parlor and sit down?"

"Well, I don't rightly know. I might get that pretty sofa of yours dirty."

Penny waved away the objection. "Don't worry about that. I want you to sit down and tell me all about what you've been doing."

As the two young people settled down on the sofa with a respectable distance between them, Penny's eyes glistened warmly when she looked at Wray. That expression was mirrored in his gaze.

Several days had passed since they had last seen each other, and Wray began relating the details of his work on McCabe's Trident ranch. Of course, half of the ranch now belonged to Penny, but Wray's tone as he spoke to her was not that of a hired hand talking to his employer. He talked of the little things that happened during his day, sharing his feelings and the flavor of his life with her. Penny listened with rapt attention.

Wray began to seem more distracted, and after several minutes he abruptly changed the subject. "I hear that Mr. McCabe came to see you yesterday." His face and voice showed no emotion.

The statement surprised Penny. "How did you know that?" she asked.

Wray shook his head. "It was just something I heard. Has he been bothering you, Miss Penny?"

"Why . . . of course not. Mr. McCabe is my business partner now, you know. It's perfectly acceptable for one partner to visit another."

"That's why he came?" Wray demanded. "To talk business?"

Penny caught her breath, and her eyes flashed angrily. Joel Wray had no right to come into her house and question her this way, no matter how he felt about her—or how she felt about him.

"What goes on between Mr. McCabe and me is none of your concern, Joel," she said firmly. "Such matters are private."

"Are they?" he growled. He moved closer to her on the sofa. "Private like that day I showed you around the ranch, and we stopped up on the west ridge?"

Penny blushed. "All right, you kissed me, and I kissed you. That doesn't give you the right to run my life."

A grin tugged at Wray's mouth, and the look in his eyes softened. "You enjoyed it," he said. "And you've let me come calling on you ever since. I reckon I can understand why you didn't want your father to know about it. I'm just a cowhand on a ranch that he owned half of, but I was starting to hope that you and me . . . Well, things are different now, and there'll come a time when you have to decide what you want out of life, Penny."

She nodded jerkily. "I know, Joel. It's just that so much has happened. It's so hard to think these days, and I keep finding out things I hadn't known. . . ."

He reached out and gently touched her arm. "I know it's been hard for you," he said softly. "I want to help any way I can."

Penny leaned toward him. That was all the encouragement he needed to slip his arms around her and embrace her. She rested her head against his shoulder for a moment, then lifted her face to his. Wray's mouth came down on hers, and as their lips met she pressed her body against him.

As he leaned back against the sofa, she rested her

head on his shoulder again. They stayed that way, comfortable with each other, for several minutes. A part of Penny wished that she could remain sheltered in Wray's arms, protected from all the confusion she felt. She wished she could forget all the blows that life had dealt her in the last few weeks, put all the questions out of her mind.

But she could not ignore all the changes that had come her way. Closing her eyes to the problems of the future would not make them go away. She sighed deeply.

Gently Wray began to stroke her hair. "What's wrong?" he asked quietly. "When I first came in here, I thought something was riding you."

Penny hesitated, then replied, "Something . . . strange happened earlier tonight. I had another visitor."

"McCabe?" Wray asked, bristling slightly.

Penny shook her head. "No, it wasn't Flint. It was Simon Smith."

Wray frowned as he tried to place the name. Finally, he said, "Isn't that the boy who works at the newspaper? The fella that's not quite right in the head?"

"Yes, that's him. But Simon's just a little slow, Joel. He's not as simpleminded as people think he is." Penny was a little surprised to find herself defending Simon. She had always felt uneasy around him and had as little to do with him as possible. She realized that his bringing the papers to her had been an uncomplicated, honest act and that she had been wrong about him all along. She was learning that things were not always as they seemed. Perhaps it was time she started giving people the benefit of the doubt more often. She went on. "He brought over some documents of my father's that he found at the newspaper office."

Wray shook his head. "That doesn't make any sense. Why would any of your father's papers be at the newspaper office? You know Miss Carson and he didn't get along at all."

"I know." Penny nodded. "I think Ruth Carson got her hands on them somehow and probably intended to use them against my father."

"Stole them, you mean?"

"I didn't want to put it quite that harshly, but yes, that's what I mean."

Wray nodded thoughtfully. "What are these documents?" he asked.

"I'll get them and show them to you." Penny went to the desk. As she opened the drawer and gathered the papers, she wondered why she was trusting Wray with this information. It had been so easy to share her troubles with him this evening, and she was tired of struggling alone. She knew that Joel Wray was a strong, honest man who genuinely cared for her, just as Penny cared for him.

Returning to the sofa, she sat down beside him and handed him the sheaf of documents. Wray took them, and as he began to study them his brow furrowed in concentration. After a few minutes, he said, "I don't know a whole lot about business, but these look like some sort of records. You say your father wrote them?"

"That's right. As far as I can tell, they give the details of some of the business deals my father and Flint were involved in. Surely since you work on the ranch you've heard of the Great Plains Cattle Company."

Wray shook his head. "I'm afraid not. This place is in Laramie. When we sell off stock, we either do it locally or drive it to the stockyards in Council Bluffs." He pointed a blunt finger at a column of numbers. "Besides, there's probably ten times the number of head listed here than we've actually sold since I've been working for Trident."

"But that doesn't make sense." Penny's blond head moved next to his as she leaned over to point to other columns on the page. "You can see how much money the partnership has made, and how much they've spent on acquiring new range."

Wray nodded, and his eyes hardened. "I can see, all right," he said grimly. "This doesn't look too good, Penny."

"What do you mean?" she demanded.

"I mean it looks to me like McCabe and your father were mixed up in something crooked," he replied flatly.

Penny stared at him for a long moment, and the look in her eyes turned icy cold. Finally she said, "That's a lie. I won't have you accusing my father of such a thing, Joel."

Wray's mouth tightened, and he shrugged his shoulders, obviously trying to keep a close rein on his temper. "I'm just going by what's written here," he said.

"My father was not a . . . a criminal," Penny insisted.

Wray nodded and stood up. "I hope not, Miss Penny." He handed her the papers. "But if I was you,

I'd hang on to those until all this gets straightened out. Whatever you do, don't give them to McCabe. Could be he was behind it, and your father didn't know a thing about it. We don't want to tip our hand."

"Tip our hand?"

The young cowboy's anger had subsided, and he was able to smile at her again. "I reckon I'll be looking into this business. Don't you worry about a thing, Penny. I plan on getting to the bottom of it."

"Would you, Joel?" She stood up and slipped a hand into his.

"Sure. You just wait and see." He bent quickly and brushed his lips against hers. "Everything's going to be fine."

But after he was gone, doubts returned to plague Penny, and she wished that Joel Wray were with her again to hold her and tell her that everything would be all right.

When Luke Travis and Joel Wray had arrived back in Cheyenne earlier and split up just before entering town, the marshal had told the young cowhand that he planned to return to his hotel. Wray did not tell Travis what his plans were. For the past several months he had been slipping into town to see Penny whenever he had a chance, and he kept his movements secret from everyone.

Wray recalled that Travis mentioned he was staying at the Barnes Hotel. After leaving the Yates house, the young man headed for the hotel, riding through Cheyenne's back streets and alleys, mulling over what he had discovered.

Abilene's marshal suspected that Flint McCabe was somehow involved with the rustling ring that was operating in the area, and what Wray had learned tonight lent weight to that theory. He knew for a fact that McCabe and Mayor Yates had been selling cattle to the livestock company in Laramie, more cattle than could have come from the Trident range. There was only one explanation for such a surplus of animals.

McCabe was stealing them.

It was possible that McCabe had been keeping Yates in the dark about the rustling, just as Wray had suggested to Penny. If that were the case, and Yates found out about it, then McCabe had another powerful reason to want his partner out of the way. The mayor might have threatened to expose his partner to the law.

Wray realized that in the short time he had known Travis, the man from Abilene had convinced him that Ruth Carson was innocent. Now he saw that Travis's hunch about the rustling being connected with Yates's murder had to be correct.

But there was no way of proving any of it, not even with the documents that Penny now had in her possession. By themselves, they did not prove a thing except that McCabe had sold some cattle—and ranchers did that all the time.

Wray found the Barnes Hotel and tied his horse in the alley behind the building. He went in through the back door, causing the clerk at the desk to look up in surprise when he stepped into the lobby from the kitchen.

"Is there a fella named Luke Travis staying here?" Wray asked.

The clerk nodded and told him the room number. "I think I saw Mr. Travis come in a little while ago. He should still be in his room."

Wray nodded his thanks and went up the stairs to the second floor. A moment later, he knocked on the door of the room. Travis's voice called, "Who is it?"

"Joel Wray."

Travis opened the door and stepped back to let Wray into the room. The young cowboy noticed that there was a gun in Travis's hand, the same walnut-butted Peacemaker that Wray had seen the lawman using so efficiently at Cue Ball. Travis went to the dresser, slid the pistol into the holster lying there with its coiled shell belt, and then turned to face his visitor. "Didn't expect to see you again so soon, Wray," Travis commented.

"I just found out something you might be interested in," Wray replied. Quickly, he told Travis about the documents Penny Yates had shown him a few minutes earlier, explaining also how she had come to have them. "I don't know where your sister-in-law got them, but from what I saw, they sure seem to indicate that McCabe was behind the rustling, just like you thought."

"Or McCabe and Yates," Travis said. He thoughtfully rubbed his jaw. "Still, if Yates wasn't supposed to know and found out accidentally, that would give McCabe a reason to get rid of him."

"That's what I thought."

A grin stretched across Travis's face. "You didn't tell me you were coming in to town tonight. Just happened to run into Penny Yates, and she happened to tell you about all this, eh?"

Wray flushed and stared down at his boots. "I think Miss Penny's a fine woman," he said.

Travis slapped his shoulder and laughed. "You

could be right, Joel. I appreciate you letting me know about this."

"What are you going to do?"

Travis considered that briefly, then said, "I've got to go to Laramie and try to find out some more about this Great Plains Cattle Company. If I can prove that McCabe and Yates were mixed up in something crooked, I might be able to get the judge to postpone the hanging while the matter is under investigation."

"Even if they were behind the rustling, that doesn't mean Miss Carson didn't poison the mayor," Wray pointed out.

"I know. But right now all I'm after is time to cast some doubt and find the real killer."

Both men knew all too well that the time Travis spoke of was running out. In only a little over two days, Ruth Carson would be hanged.

"How long do you think it'll take me to ride to Laramie and back?" the marshal asked. "You know the country around here better than I do."

Wray nodded and smiled. "I reckon it'll take *us* about two days if we get a good start early tomorrow."

Travis cocked an eyebrow. "Us?"

"Like you said, I know the country. And you're liable to be riding into trouble, too. You might run into Doak Lawton and his men again."

Travis studied the young man for a moment. "It hasn't been twelve hours since we first ran into each other, Joel. In that time, because of me, you've been shot at a couple of times and beaten by a bunch of hardcases who wanted to stomp you into the ground. You don't owe me a thing. How'd you wind up on my side of this fight?"

Wray grinned. "Hell, you're in the right, aren't you?" He stuck out his hand. "I've never had much of a chance to do anything except punch cattle, Marshal. Lots of folks can do that. I figure this is my opportunity to do something a little more worthwhile."

Travis took Wray's hand and shook it firmly. "Glad to have you with me," he said sincerely. "Like you said, though, there's liable to be some gunplay."

"I'm up to it," Wray said with a short laugh.

"What about your job?" Travis asked. "Doesn't McCabe take exception to his riders traipsing all over the country and not taking care of their work?"

"I wouldn't worry about that," Wray assured him. "McCabe can fire me if he wants to, that's up to him. Besides, the more I find out about Flint McCabe, the less I want to work for him."

And the less likely that Penny Yates would give in to her fears and uncertainties and let McCabe buffalo her into marrying him, Wray added silently to himself.

Chapter Eleven

WEDNESDAY MORNING DAWNED GRAY AND OVERCAST IN Cheyenne. Dark, leaden clouds shrouded the Laramie Mountains, and the craggy peaks were lost in a swirling mist. As P. K. Nelson glanced out of his hotel-room window, he thought it was the perfect day for the mood he was in.

Keeping one eye on the weather, he dressed slowly. If it began to rain, he would not be able to put the finishing touches on the gallows. Of course, he had planned to complete the work with over a day and a half to spare so that even if a storm delayed him today, Ruth Carson's execution would probably still take place on schedule.

Nelson secretly hoped that nature would somehow sense the injustice of the situation and take steps to stop it, at least for a while.

When he left the hotel after breakfast, however,

Nelson discovered that the wind was out of the south. It was carrying the clouds past Cheyenne, taking them harmlessly to the east of the town. Nelson looked up, saw the overcast shredding and blowing away, and spotted patches of blue sky. He grimaced.

The hangman started walking toward the courthouse but along the way decided to detour slightly to the sheriff's office. When he entered, he found Dehner sitting at his desk, sipping a cup of coffee.

"Mornin'," the sheriff grunted as Nelson closed the door behind him. "Care for a cup of coffee?"

Nelson shook his head. "No, thanks. I just had breakfast at the hotel dining room."

"Jeremy tells me you came by and had quite a little talk with the prisoner last night."

Nelson stiffened. "The boy told me he didn't eavesdrop. I figured I could believe him."

"You figured right," Dehner grunted. "He's my nephew, and besides that he's a damned good deputy. He didn't listen in, he just said that you were back there talking to Miss Carson for quite a while." The lawman eyed Nelson speculatively. "If you don't mind my asking, what is it with you, mister? Is it that she's a woman, and you've never hung a woman before?"

Nelson bristled. "Judge Shaw called me in because I'm the best there is at my business, Sheriff. Hanging a woman is going to cause quite a stir. Over the next couple of days people are going to be coming into Cheyenne from all over the territory to see it. The judge doesn't want anything to go wrong."

"That doesn't answer my question," Dehner pointed out.

"I've always done my job the best way I know how.

I'll do my duty as the judge and jury decreed it. But that doesn't mean I'm convinced Ruth Carson is guilty. I don't think that lady ever deliberately hurt anybody."

With an exasperated sigh Dehner placed his palms on the desk and shoved himself to his feet. "You and that damned Travis!" he snapped. "I heard he was in the Golden Gate district a couple of nights ago, asking all sorts of questions about rustling and Flint McCabe and God knows what else. You'd think that a man like Travis would have faith in the legal system." Dehner's pointed look made it clear he thought the same thing about Nelson. "He came by here awful damn early this morning and talked to his sister-in-law for a few minutes. Didn't look too happy when he left."

The hangman shrugged. "I don't imagine he is. Travis isn't convinced of Ruth's guilt, and neither am I. I intend to go over to Judge Shaw's office today and review the records of the trial with him. Maybe the jury overlooked something in the testimony."

"I was there, Nelson," the sheriff said firmly, glaring at him. "It was a fair trial, and all the evidence was brought out. I don't know what else any of us could be expected to do."

Nelson met the sheriff's stare, then said abruptly, "Can I talk to Miss Carson again?"

"Sure, why not? She's probably finished her breakfast by now, so I'll need to get her tray, anyway."

Dehner unlocked the cellblock door and stepped into the hall. "Got a visitor for you again, Miss Ruth," he said.

Ruth glanced up from the copy of the *Eagle* she was reading. When she saw Nelson, she folded the paper and put it on the bunk, then came to the bars to greet him. "Good morning, Mr. Nelson," she said pleasantly.

Sweeping off his hat, Nelson nodded and said, "Miss Carson. I trust you're feeling well this morning."

"As well as can be expected," she replied.

"I'm going back to the office," Dehner said warily. "Bang on the door when you're finished, Nelson."

"Your deputy was a little worried that I might decide to give the prisoner a gun, Sheriff," Nelson said. "Maybe you'd better search me."

Dehner laughed harshly. "Jeremy's still a boy in some ways, Nelson. You know I'd shoot any prisoner who tried to escape. You're not stupid enough to risk such a thing."

"True enough." Nelson inclined his head in agreement.

Once Dehner had left with the breakfast tray, Nelson put his hat on the three-legged stool and extended a hand through the bars to Ruth. She hesitated for a moment, then took it. Nelson rested his other hand on top of hers. "I'm going to do everything I can to prevent this travesty of justice, Miss Carson. I promise you that."

Ruth smiled thinly. "You mean you'll do everything you can *legally*. If nothing has changed by nine o'clock Friday morning, you'll carry out the sentence of the court, won't you, Mr. Nelson?"

Her cool, slightly mocking voice cut him like a knife. "I've always done my job," he replied. "I . . . I don't know if I can do anything else, ma'am."

"I can respect that." Ruth nodded. "I've always done my job, too. It's important to me." She slipped her hand from his grasp, turned to the bunk, and picked up the paper. "That's why it bothers me to see Malcolm make such mistakes," she said, pointing to the page. "Here, look at this. The print is crooked, and three words are misspelled in this edition. Would you do something for me, Mr. Nelson?"

"Of course, dear lady."

"Would you speak to Malcolm and tell him that I expect more attention to detail from him in the future? No matter whether I'm here or not, the masthead of the *Eagle* will always say 'Founded by R. Carson.' I want that to appear only on a newspaper I could be proud of."

Nelson drew a deep breath. "Certainly, I'll speak to the young man. But couldn't you tell him yourself? Surely he comes here to see you."

Ruth shook her head. "He did at first. Now, he's so depressed and frustrated by his inability to help me that I don't think he could stand to see me. He hasn't been by in several days."

"I'll definitely have a talk with him," Nelson said sternly. Then he went on. "The sheriff said your brother-in-law paid you a visit earlier. Has he had any luck in his investigation?"

"I'm . . . not sure. Luke was rather closemouthed this morning, but he seemed excited about something. He said he had to make a short trip but that I shouldn't worry. He would be back before Friday morning."

Nelson frowned, surprised that Travis would be leaving Cheyenne at this time. He supposed Travis had a good reason, but it was still puzzling. "Did he say where he was going?"

"No, just that he had turned up something he wanted to look at more closely." For the first time,

Nelson heard the iron control in Ruth's voice slip as she continued. "I wish he hadn't left. I know he's just trying to help me, but it seemed to make me feel better, just knowing he was here."

Nelson felt his chest tighten, and he suddenly wished Ruth was expressing those sentiments about *him.*

He took her hand again. "I'm sure Luke is doing the right thing. I got to know him pretty well during the train trip out here, you know, and he struck me as a very competent man. He's going to do anything he sets his mind to. And in the meantime, I'm going over to talk to Judge Shaw today, just as soon as—" He broke off abruptly, catching himself before he could finish the sentence.

"As soon as you finish my gallows, you started to say," said Ruth, finishing it for him. That cool smile of hers curved her lips. "Don't worry, Mr. Nelson. I don't harbor any ill feeling toward you. As you told me, you're just doing your job."

Nelson said nothing. But as he looked at her, he knew that for the first time in his career, just doing his job would not answer the questions that were plaguing him.

And also for the first time, he knew that when the moment arrived, he might not be able to pull that fatal lever.

Luke Travis had been tempted to start for Laramie the night before, rather than waiting until morning, but Joel Wray had convinced him it would be better to wait. Both Wray's horse and Travis's rented mount were tired from the trip to Cue Ball.

Travis then began to think of other ways of getting

there. He checked with the desk clerk and found that the next train bound for Laramie did not pass through Cheyenne until Wednesday night, and there was no stagecoach until Friday. Horseback was the only way to reach Laramie and possibly make it back to Cheyenne by nine o'clock Friday morning.

Travis slept very little on Tuesday night, and he was up and ready to pull out by dawn. Joel Wray appeared at the livery stable where they had agreed to meet a little after six. All that was left for Travis to do was pick up some jerky and biscuits for the trip. He hated to leave Ruth at a time like this, but if he was successful in exposing McCabe's part in the rustling ring, that might mean more to her than anything he could do in Cheyenne.

By the time the dark clouds scudded away to the east, Travis and Wray were several miles west of town. Both men kept an eye on the storm, knowing that it could slow them down. But the clouds moved on and then broke up, and the two men found themselves riding through a glorious sunlit morning with a cool breeze fanning their cheeks.

"I've been thinking, Marshal," Joel Wray mused. "It strikes me as strange that Trident would have been losing stock right along if McCabe and Yates were behind the rustling."

Travis shook his head. "Nothing strange about that. McCabe's no fool, Joel. He knows that if his ranch isn't hit by the thieves the same as everybody else's, he'd be under suspicion right away. Chances are he just has Lawton haze off some Trident cattle every now and then to make things look good."

"Reckon it could work that way, all right. I'd sure like to prove that McCabe's mixed up in all this."

The marshal glanced over at the young cowhand and saw the intensity on his face. Wray was proving to be a valuable ally. Even though his motives were different from Travis's, they were both working toward the same goal. Travis would have been willing to bet that Wray's reasons for joining him had something to do with Penny Yates. The marshal could understand that. Penny was a lovely young woman with a lot of spirit. She was probably pretty spoiled, but with the right man pulling in double harness with her, she would be all right.

The two men kept their horses moving at a fast walk, a ground-eating gait that would not tire them too much or too quickly. Travis had to keep a grip on his impatience. He knew how important this journey to Laramie was. He had not been able to find any other leads that might save Ruth's life, and this trip would take up all the time remaining to her. The results of this mission would either save her—or Travis would have failed abysmally.

As they rode, Wray asked questions about Kansas, and Travis told him about life in Abilene. Wray commented that it sounded like a good place to live. "It is," Travis agreed. "And we do everything we can to keep it that way."

Since the road was broad and fairly level, it was easy to make good time. Travis and Wray paused for lunch at a café in a small settlement about a quarter of the way between Cheyenne and Laramie. They also watered their horses and let the animals rest for a while, and they were back on the trail fairly quickly.

Travis had always thought that spending time with a man on the trail was the best way to get to know him. During the afternoon, Joel Wray told him about growing up on the Texas frontier and learning to fight Kiowas and Comanches before he was a dozen years old. He was also taught early how to ride a horse, use a rope, and persuade stubborn cattle to go where he wanted. When the great trail drives began after the Civil War, it seemed perfectly natural to Wray to be a part of them.

"Never made it into Abilene," he said. "The men I rode for always took their herds into Caldwell or Newton or Dodge. I kept hearing about Wyoming, and when I decided it was time to drift, this was where I headed. I haven't regretted it yet."

"It is pretty country," Travis agreed, looking toward the mountains.

"It's a land where a man can really make something for himself," Wray said fervently. "If he's got the right woman, and if the big ranchers will give him a chance, there's no limit to what he can do."

"You sound like you've got some plans."

Wray grinned. "Most men do. Some just aren't willing to work as hard for them as I am."

Travis could believe that. Wray struck him as a young man who would not give up until he had what he wanted out of life.

They ate a light supper on the trail, pausing only long enough to rest the horses. Travis did not mind the jerky and the hard biscuits. He was too acutely aware of the passage of time to care about what he ate.

The sun sank behind the mountains, and still the two men rode on. Wray estimated that they would reach Laramie sometime after ten. First thing in the morning, they would hunt for the Great Plains Cattle Company's offices and find out if what they suspected was true. Then there would be the long hard ride back to Cheyenne. With any luck they would return several hours before the hanging.

That was trusting an awful lot to luck, Travis thought grimly. But there was nothing else he could do, short of trying to rescue Ruth by force. And he was not sure he could bring himself to do that. Upholding the law was an ideal deeply ingrained in him.

The night was clear and bright, with the moon and stars providing enough light to allow them to see the road. From time to time a few wispy clouds floated in front of the moon and blocked its light, but overall the sky was clear. Even though it was summer, the wind picked up, and the night became colder. The crisp bite in the air reminded them that they were on the edge of the high country.

After hours of riding through the darkness, Travis spotted the lights of Laramie ahead. He wanted to urge his horse to a trot, but he knew that insisting on such a pace would be cruel to both exhausted animals. And there was really no reason to rush at this hour. It was unlikely they would find anyone who could give them any information.

The saloons were still open and doing a good business as Travis and Wray rode down Laramie's main street. At this hour they were the only establishments still open. Travis peered through the moonlight and studied the names of the businesses they passed. They had gone several blocks when he suddenly pointed and said, "There."

THE GREAT PLAINS CATTLE COMPANY, the letters arranged in an arch, was painted on one of the storefront windows. The narrow single-story building was wedged between a barber shop and a mercantile. The office was dark inside, but the light coming from the saloon across the street shone on the sign on the window. The noises coming from the saloon—tinny music, the stomping of boots on the floor, and laughter from both men and women—were all too familiar.

Travis and Wray reined in their horses in front of the cattle company and exchanged a glance. "We won't have any trouble finding it in the morning," Travis said. He inclined his head toward the saloon. "You want a drink?"

"I'd rather have some sleep," Wray said. "The last couple of days have been pretty busy."

"That they have," Travis agreed. He felt weariness overtaking him. "Let's go find a stable for the horses and a hotel for us."

Wray grinned. "Sounds good."

As the two men rode down the street, both of them wondered just what the morning would bring.

Chapter Twelve

THERE WAS NO CHANCE OF RAIN THURSDAY MORNING, P. K. Nelson saw as he walked to the courthouse. It was a beautiful day except for the heat. The cool breezes of the day before were gone, leaving behind a warmth that soon threatened to grow oppressive.

It would be even hotter inside the jail, Nelson knew. The single window in Ruth Carson's cell would not allow much air into that small space.

Nelson paused on the edge of the wide lawn in front of the courthouse. The gallows stood starkly framed against the bright blue sky, the harsh sunlight casting its clearly defined shadow on the ground. Quite a few people were standing around the courthouse square, gaping at the gallows and muttering amongst themselves. A feeling of excitement and anticipation filled the air.

The hangman had seen the same thing many times

before. A hanging brought people into town from miles around. Some folks thought nothing of riding a hundred miles to witness an execution. That said something about the loneliness and grinding boredom of life on much of the frontier. In this case, with the added novelty of an attractive woman being involved, it was likely that scores of people would pour into Cheyenne today, camping out overnight so as to have a good spot in the morning.

Nelson had never cared for the carnival atmosphere that went with this part of his job. He liked a good joke as much as anybody else—even more than most folks, he thought—but when it came down to the actual executions, those were serious business. Anyway, he had not felt much like joking since he had arrived in Cheyenne and met Ruth Carson. No, this was not a laughing matter at all.

A man wearing a deputy's badge was standing near the base of the gallows, a rifle cradled loosely in his arms. Sheriff Dehner had deputized several of the townsmen and given them the job of guarding the gallows, more to keep mischievous children from bothering it than from any worry about sabotage. Nelson walked up to the deputy now on duty and nodded a greeting to him. "Any trouble?" he asked.

"No, sir, Mr. Nelson," the man replied. He had also been one of the laborers who had constructed the scaffold under Nelson's supervision. "There's been plenty of folks takin' a gander at this here gallows, but ain't nobody tried to bother it."

"Good," Nelson grunted. He went over to the steps—thirteen of them, of course—and climbed up to the platform. From here he could look out over the town and see the wagons and horses streaming through the streets, bringing in the curious to witness tomorrow's hanging.

He put his hand on the trapdoor lever, sighing as he rested it there. Everything had gone well during the final stages of the gallows' construction the day before. The lever and the bars that it controlled worked perfectly, assuring that the opening of the trapdoor would be smooth. Later Nelson would test it again one more time, just to be sure, but he knew it was not really necessary. Ruth Carson would not cheat the gallows because of mechanical failure.

Nor could Nelson do anything from the legal end. He had spent long hours the day before with Judge Franklin Shaw, studying the records of the trial. After he completed his careful review, Nelson had to agree with the judge and Sheriff Dehner: The trial had seemed fair, the testimony complete.

As he let his gaze rove over the town, Nelson spotted the office of the *Cheyenne Eagle* a couple of blocks away. Its sign, with its distinctive likeness of an eagle in flight, was hard to miss. Seeing it reminded him of his promise to Ruth to speak to her assistant, Malcolm Ebersole. Thinking of that made Nelson's face set in stern lines. He did not know Ebersole, but the young man should have come by the jail to see Ruth. He should not have turned his back on her in her time of trouble, no matter how upset he was by the situation.

Nelson nodded to himself. He had been too busy the day before, but he would pay a visit to Ebersole right now.

* * *

"You *what?*" The angry voice cracked through the newspaper office. "Dammit, Simon, whatever possessed you to do that?"

Simon Smith shuffled his feet uneasily and rubbed his eyebrows, staring at the floor as he listened to Malcolm Ebersole's sharp words. Ebersole stood opposite the young man and glared at him, his eyes glittering with rage.

"I'm sorry, Mr. Ebersole," Simon finally summoned up the courage to say. "I . . . I just thought it might be a good idea to clean up around here. You know how Miss Ruth always says the newspaper business is messy enough as it is, that you oughtn't to have any more clutter around than you have to. When I found them papers behind the drawer in the desk, I just figured I'd better get rid of 'em. I meant to tell you before now, but I guess I sort of forgot."

Ebersole took a deep breath and made an obvious effort to control his temper. "I know Miss Ruth said that, Simon, but that doesn't give you the right to go through the office and dispose of things yourself."

"But I didn't throw nothing away!" Simon protested. "I just took them papers back to Miss Penny, since they belonged to her daddy."

"Those documents didn't belong to Yates anymore." Ebersole's self-control deserted him as his anger flared again. "Didn't you stop to think that they were there for a reason, you stupid fool?"

Ebersole's voice was loud now, and he did not hear the door of the office opening. Simon's eyes were still downcast.

The first hint either of them had that a third person was in the room was the sound of someone clearing his throat. "Ah, excuse me," a deep voice said. "I'm looking for Malcolm Ebersole."

"I'm Ebersole," he said, swinging around, instantly composed. He saw a burly figure in a derby and a suit standing just inside the doorway and watching them with a cool gaze. Ebersole went on. "What can I do for you?"

"I have a message for you, Mr. Ebersole," P. K. Nelson said. "From Miss Ruth Carson."

Ebersole's manner changed even more. He swept a stack of newsprint off a chair next to a desk and thrust it into Simon's arms, then turned the chair to face Nelson. "Please, come in and have a seat, sir," he said. "Are you a friend of Ruth's?"

"You might say that," Nelson replied as he settled into the chair. "My name is P. K. Nelson."

Ebersole frowned. "Nelson, Nelson," he mused. "That name seems familiar. . . ." He stiffened as he recalled where he had heard the name. The friendliness he had shown a moment earlier vanished as he growled, "What the hell do you want here, Nelson? Don't you have any sense of decency?"

"I like to think I do," Nelson said, keeping a tight rein on his own emotions. "You obviously know who I am, Mr. Ebersole, so I won't bother trying to explain. But Miss Carson *did* send me over to see you, and you could confirm that yourself if you'd just pay her a visit."

Ebersole flushed at Nelson's scolding tone. He looked up and saw Simon watching them, his mouth slightly open. Waving his arm impatiently, Ebersole snapped, "Go on, Simon. Take that newsprint back to the storeroom. We don't need it right now." When the young man was gone, Ebersole looked back at Nelson and went on. "All right, mister, if you've got something to say, you say it and then get out of here."

"All right," Nelson replied stiffly. Quickly, he conveyed the concerns about the paper that Ruth had mentioned to him. Ebersole became more angry as he listened, but when Nelson had finished, Ebersole put his hands on his hips, drew a deep breath, and heaved a sigh.

"Ruth's right," he said wearily. "I should have gone to see her more often, and I should have been paying more attention to the details here at the paper. I've just been so damned upset about this whole thing—" He broke off and shook his head. "But I don't guess you'd understand that, would you?"

"As a matter of fact, I do," Nelson replied, his own voice more friendly now. "You see, Mr. Ebersole, I don't believe that Ruth is guilty, either." He hesitated a moment. "In fact, I've grown rather fond of her. So you can understand the dilemma I find myself in now."

"Of course." Ebersole sank down in the chair behind the desk opposite Nelson. "It's complete lunacy to think that Ruth could kill anyone. But the evidence is so overwhelming. What can anybody do?" Resignation was plain in his voice and on his face.

"I happen to know that Luke Travis is trying to find some way of clearing Ruth's name," Nelson said.

Ebersole nodded. "Travis came by here a couple of days ago and talked to me. I didn't know what I could tell him that would help. In fact, I haven't seen him since then."

"I'm sure he's doing his best. That's all any of us can do." Nelson put his hands on his knees and stood up. He paused, then nodded toward the door of the storeroom where Simon had disappeared. "Speaking of that, weren't you being a little hard on that young man when I came in? I don't know what he did, and it's none of my business, but he doesn't seem the type to deserve such a dressing-down."

Ebersole smiled sheepishly. "You're right. I guess I did fly off the handle. Simon just got a little carried away with some cleaning up around here and got rid of something he shouldn't have."

"Documents belonging to the late Mayor Yates, I believe you said." Nelson smiled. "I didn't mean to eavesdrop as I came in, but I did happen to overhear that much."

Ebersole shook his head. "I'm not even sure what they were myself. I imagine it was some research Ruth had done for a story. But I'm downright certain there couldn't have been anything of Yates's here in this office."

"You wouldn't think so," Nelson agreed. He extended his hand to Ebersole. "Well, I'm glad to meet you, Mr. Ebersole. I just hope you'll have some good news to write about tomorrow."

"So do I, Mr. Nelson," Ebersole said fervently as he shook the hangman's hand. "So do I."

Nelson was deep in thought as he left the newspaper office. He had been a bit embarrassed to interrupt the angry scene he walked in on, but it gave him some more to chew on. If young Simon was correct, Ruth had had documents belonging to Mayor Yates in her possession. That was unlikely, Nelson knew, but if that had been the case, what did it mean?

Maybe there was more to this than anyone had

realized yet. Nelson's steps took him toward the jail. He wanted to have another talk with Ruth.

When Nelson entered the sheriff's office, he found the young deputy, Jeremy, on duty. He greeted Nelson with a polite smile, then said, "I reckon you want to see Miss Ruth again."

"If that's all right," Nelson replied.

"I guess it would be." Jeremy's face became solemn. "You know, I never knew Miss Ruth until, well, until she was a prisoner, but I hate to see this happen to her. She seems like too nice a lady to be hanged."

Nelson sighed. "I couldn't agree with you more, Jeremy. Now, if I could talk to her for a few minutes?"

"Sure." Jeremy unlocked the cellblock door for Nelson, then closed it behind him.

Ruth was sitting in the rocking chair. She smiled up at her visitor and said, "Good morning, Mr. Nelson."

"Phineas," he said.

"I beg your pardon?"

"Phineas." He pulled over the stool and sat down in front of the bars. "It's my first name. I usually just use my initials because folks seem to think that Phineas Kingsley Nelson is a funny name. But I don't mind my friends using it."

A faint smile curved Ruth's lips. "And you regard me as one of your friends, Phineas?" she asked dryly.

"I hope so."

"I'm afraid it's going to be a friendship of rather short duration."

"Now, don't talk like that, blast it!" Nelson exclaimed. "Travis isn't back yet. I'm sure he's going to return with some sort of evidence to clear you."

"I'm afraid it would be wishful thinking to believe

so," Ruth replied. "But I'm glad you haven't lost hope. As for me, I think I'm just going to have to resign myself to my fate. It will be easier that way."

Nelson's roiling emotions would not let him sit still. He stood up and began pacing back and forth in the short hall. Even though he had known her only briefly, he knew that it was not like Ruth Carson to give up. Sharing with him the true depth of her despair told him she had abandoned hope.

He stopped his pacing and grasped the bars of the cell door. "I went by the newspaper office and had that talk with your assistant, Ebersole. I think he'll be more careful about details in the future."

Ruth smiled again. "How is Malcolm? I hope he's bearing up all right."

"He seemed pretty upset, but I imagine he'll be all right."

"What about Simon? Did you see him?"

Nelson nodded. "I didn't talk to him, but he was there."

"I've been especially worried about Simon. Malcolm is an intelligent, ambitious young man. He may be upset now, but he'll get over it and make a success of himself. Simon was so much more dependent on me. He's a very sweet boy, Phineas, and the people in this town just never understood him. They never even dreamed how much talent he has."

Nelson remembered the lumbering way Simon had carried the newsprint out of the office and the vacant look he had in his eyes until Ebersole had given him his orders. "What sort of talent does a lad like that have?" he asked, puzzled.

Pride gleamed in Ruth's eyes. "Did you notice the eagle painted on our sign?" she asked.

"Of course. It's magnificent."

"Simon painted it. He has a great deal of natural artistic ability."

Nelson frowned in surprise. He would never have guessed that the young man possessed such a talent.

"One day I found him sketching on some newsprint with a piece of charcoal," Ruth went on. "I started to scold him for wasting the paper, and then I saw what he had drawn. It was a lovely scene from the Laramie Mountains. From that day on I encouraged his drawing and painting. With someone to help him, to look out for his interests, he might be able to make a career of it someday." She lifted her shoulders in a tiny shrug and smiled. "I had hoped to be able to help him myself. That's one of the things I regret most about this whole affair."

Nelson said nothing for a long moment, uncertain how to reply to Ruth's poignant comment. Finally, he told her, "When I got there, Ebersole was upset with Simon about some documents he had found and taken to Mayor Yates's daughter. Did you have some papers belonging to Yates, Ruth?"

She frowned. "Documents? What kind of documents?"

"I have no idea. All I know is that Ebersole was quite angry because Simon found the papers and took them to Miss Yates."

Ruth shook her head. "I don't know what you're talking about, Phineas. I would have liked to get my hands on something other than the public records concerning Yates. Perhaps if I had, I could have proved that Yates and McCabe were involved in something illegal." She laughed shortly. "I might have even won the election then."

Nelson sighed. Far from being the straightforward job he had expected when he received Judge Shaw's wire, this matter was becoming more complicated with every day that passed.

"I had better go before young Jeremy out there starts to get nervous," he said. "I'll see you again, Ruth."

"I know. In the morning at nine o'clock, isn't it?"

Nelson scowled. *How could she be so blasted flippant about it?* But that might be the only way she could maintain control, he realized.

"I'll see you before then," he said quietly. He went to the cellblock door and rapped on it.

Jeremy let him out and made some comment to him as he left the office, but Nelson did not hear the young man's words. He was too preoccupied with everything that had happened during the last few days. He was only vaguely aware of the people he passed on the streets and barely noticed that even more people were in Cheyenne now than had been there earlier.

Not surprisingly, Nelson's steps led him back to the gallows. Another deputy had relieved the one who had been on duty earlier. This man also recognized the hangman and let him pass unchallenged. Nelson climbed up to the platform and rested his hands on the railing.

His normally jovial face was creased in concentration. He was thinking about all the things he had discovered since arriving in Cheyenne. He had met Ruth Carson and experienced feelings he had never known before. And he had seen that not all criminal cases that were brought to trial were simple or cut-and-dried. In this instance, several issues bubbled under the surface—a handful of shadowy facts that darted about, making no sense and confusing what had seemed so obvious at first.

Nelson clenched his teeth as doubts assailed him. He turned away from the railing, strode distractedly across the platform, and gripped the trapdoor lever, his hand closing tightly on the familiar instrument. If there were so many questions about the truth in this case, he thought, what about all the other cases that were resolved with him throwing levers like this and ending a man's life in one sharp plummet?

He was convinced that Ruth Carson was innocent. *God, how many other innocent people had he sent to their death?*

As that horrible thought seered through his brain, the muscles in his arm convulsed. Without thinking, he savagely shoved the lever forward, pushing it beyond its limits. The apparatus, so carefully constructed, gave a sudden sharp crack.

The sound snapped Nelson back to his senses. He blinked, shook his head, and looked down at the broken lever in his hand. From below, the startled guard called, "Something wrong, Mr. Nelson?"

Nelson hesitated as he stared at the damage he had done. The craftsman within him was shocked by what he saw. He had always treated his work with the care and respect it deserved. But things were changing now, changing with such dizzying speed that he could no longer keep up with them.

He dropped the broken lever on the platform and strode purposefully over to the stairs. As he went down the thirteen steps, he said to the surprised guard, "I was checking the mechanism, and it failed on me. Damned if I understand why it happened, but it's got to be repaired."

The deputy gaped at him. "You mean we're goin' to have to postpone the hangin'?" he asked.

Nelson shook his head. "No, no. The damage is pretty bad, but I can still have everything ready to go in the morning. You'd better tell Sheriff Dehner about it, though. I'll keep an eye on the gallows until you get back."

"Sure." The man bobbed his head and then scurried away toward the sheriff's office.

Nelson ducked underneath the platform and craned his neck to study the arrangement of bars and hinges that would trip the trapdoor. Not only was the lever broken, but the force he had put into his push had also cracked some of the underpinnings. Still, as he had told the deputy, it was nothing that could not be repaired in time.

The hangman stayed where he was for a long time, even though it was cramped and uncomfortable under the gallows, and stared at his handiwork.

Chapter Thirteen

LUKE TRAVIS HAD ALMOST FORGOTTEN WHAT IT WAS LIKE
to get a good night's sleep. He tossed and turned most
of the night. His restlessness was not caused by the
lumpiness of the narrow bed in his hotel room but by
his impatience to be questioning whoever was in
charge of the Great Plains Cattle Company.

He was pushing himself harder than ever before,
and he was not as young as he had once been. But soon
it would be over—one way or another. At last, an hour
or so before dawn on Thursday morning, his turbulent
thoughts were overcome by sheer exhaustion, and he
dozed off.

Travis awoke a couple of hours later, shook off
the grogginess that gripped him, and went to the
room next door to get Joel Wray out of bed. The
young cowboy was equally tired. The two men found
a small café two doors away from the hotel and or-

dered a pot of coffee and a large breakfast of ham, eggs, and hotcakes. By the time they had finished eating, Travis was beginning to feel somewhat better.

"Let's get over to that office," he said as he and Wray stepped onto the boardwalk in front of the café. "Somebody ought to be there by now."

They walked down the street toward the Great Plains Cattle Company. Laramie was not as large a town as Cheyenne, but it was a growing, bustling settlement. Located on the Laramie River, it had begun as a jumble of tents and shanties during the construction of the Union Pacific Railroad. When the construction crews moved west with the railroad, a handful of settlers remained to establish the town, and it was now a shipping and supply center for the ranches in the area. Laramie was young enough that some of its businesses were still housed in tents. The sounds of sawing and hammering rang in the air this morning as the industrious new residents put up more permanent structures.

Travis figured that the Great Plains Cattle Company, wedged in a row of frame buildings, had been established and doing business for a while. As Wray and he went down the rough plank boardwalk toward it, they noticed a man approaching from the opposite direction. He reached the door of the office before they did and drew a key from his coat pocket. Unlocking the door, he swung it open just as Travis and Wray came up to him.

When they stopped at the doorway, the man nodded to them and said, "Morning, gents. Something I can do for you?"

"We're looking for whoever runs the Great Plains

Cattle Company," Travis told him. "I figure that would be you."

"Yep. Come on inside."

The broad-shouldered man led the way into the office and went to a rolltop desk that stood against one wall. He took off his cream-colored Stetson and hung it on a hook on the wall, revealing thick silvery hair. He was in his late fifties with a body that had been powerful at one time but was now shrunken with age. His lined, tanned face spoke of years spent on the range. He sank into the chair at the desk and waved to Travis and Wray to be seated in a couple of straight chairs that stood next to it.

"Name's Gordon Lutz," he told them. "What can I do for you boys?"

Travis did the talking. "Mr. Lutz," he said, "my name is Luke Travis. I'm the marshal of Abilene, Kansas, but I'm up here in Wyoming Territory on a special job." That was true, Travis thought, even though it did sound as though he had some sort of official status. "I'm looking into some transactions that have taken place through your company."

Lutz frowned. "It ain't my company, Mr. Travis. I just run it for the syndicate back in Kansas City that owns it. But I ain't sure I like the sound of what you just said. Are you implying that this outfit's not on the up-and-up?"

Travis shook his head. He had pondered that very question for quite a while. Even if McCabe was behind the wide-scale rustling that had been plaguing the Cheyenne area, that did not mean the company that had been buying the stolen cattle was aware of it. Travis said, "That's not what I meant at all. I just want to know about some cattle you've been buying." He wished he had the records that were now in Penny Yates's possession. From what Joel Wray had told him, he could pinpoint the dates and amounts of the transactions with those documents in hand. He waited while Lutz considered what he had said.

The older man mulled it over for a moment, then nodded and said, "Ask your questions, Marshal. I ain't promising I'll answer 'em, though."

"Fair enough. Do you know a man named Flint McCabe?"

Lutz shrugged his wide shoulders. "Heard the name. Big rancher down south of here, ain't he?"

"That's right. How about Roland Yates?"

"His name's familiar, too," Lutz said after a moment. "Can't rightly place him, though."

"Doak Lawton?"

"Oh, sure." Lutz grinned. "Everybody hereabouts knows Lawton. Most folks steer clear of him, though; he's got a reputation as a tough one, and he's sort of touchy, too. But I never had problems dealing with him."

"You've done business with him?"

Lutz waved a big, callused hand. "Sure. Bought plenty of cattle from him. Say, he works for that fella McCabe you mentioned, don't he?"

Travis sat up straighter, his interest quickening. "What makes you say that?"

"Well, I recollect that Lawton's brought several herds in with McCabe's brand on 'em. Trident, ain't that it?"

Joel Wray spoke for the first time. "Just the Trident brand, or were there others?" he asked sharply.

Lutz looked a little uneasy. "Well, the way it was told to me, all the spreads down that way would put their stock together for a drive now and then and use Trident as a road brand. Lawton and his crew ride for McCabe whenever he puts one of these drives together."

Travis studied the dealer's weathered face. Lutz was an old hand in the cattle business; he would have had no trouble seeing through Lawton's story concerning trail drives and road brands. But Lawton could have made it worth his while to ignore the different brands and accept the story at face value.

The marshal took a deep breath, and his face grew grim and hard. "I think you've got good records of all the dealings you've had with Lawton and McCabe," he said coldly.

"I never met McCabe," Lutz said quickly. "I was just going by what Lawton told me. Ain't never had no reason to doubt him."

The old man was part of the scheme, Travis decided, at least on the edge of it. He exchanged a glance with Wray that told him the cowboy had reached the same conclusion.

Improvising, Wray said, "Where might we find a judge in this town, mister?"

Lutz licked his lips nervously. Travis had not introduced Wray when they came in. For all Lutz knew, Wray could be a range detective or even a federal marshal. "What do you want a judge for?" he asked tensely.

"We may need a warrant sworn out," Travis replied. He had to suppress a grin. Wray was quick on the uptake, and he had played his part well.

Lutz shuffled some of the papers on his desk. "Listen, boys," he said anxiously, "you don't need no warrant to get me to cooperate. I always try to uphold law and order. Anything you need to know, you just ask."

"How about copies of the records concerning all the deals you've had with Lawton?"

"All the cattle deals, you mean?"

"Sure." Travis smile thinly. "What else could I mean?"

Lutz swallowed and started rustling through the papers even more quickly.

It took the greater part of the morning for Lutz to write out the duplicate records, but when Travis and Wray left the office of the Great Plains Cattle Company, they had a thick sheaf of papers confirming that Doak Lawton had sold thousands of head of cattle to the company over the past eighteen months. Lutz retracted his claim that he recognized only McCabe's name, as he had said at first, and admitted that Lawton had been acting as McCabe's agent in the stock transactions. Everything was a long way from being resolved, but Travis felt better as he tucked the documents inside his coat.

"That old man's part of it," Wray said as they walked toward the livery stable. "I'd stake my life on that."

"Sure he is," Travis agreed. "McCabe and Lawton paid him off. With the owners of the company back in Kansas City, Lutz probably figured nobody would ever look at things out here closely enough to call him on it."

"McCabe didn't cover his tracks too well. You saw right through that tall tale about the rustlers stealing Trident stock along with all the others."

Travis snorted. "McCabe struck me as the sort who

wouldn't think it was necessary to be too careful. He figured he had this whole territory in his back pocket. As long as he wasn't too obvious about it, nobody was going to do much sniffing in his direction."

"Then you came to Cheyenne," Wray said with a short laugh.

"That's right." Travis smiled.

The two men stopped at the hotel to pick up the saddlebags they had left in their rooms, then walked to the livery stable to get their horses. They had what they had come for, proof that Flint McCabe had sold a lot of cattle in the last year and a half. It was time to depart from Laramie.

As they were saddling up their mounts, Wray said grimly, "Reckon Penny will have to listen to reason now. There's no way I can let her marry McCabe. She'll change her thinking when she finds out he's a no-good rustler."

Travis shook his head. "We don't have any proof of that."

Wray frowned and gestured toward Travis's coat pocket. "What about those records?"

"They just confirm what we suspected about those papers Simon Smith found," Travis pointed out. "McCabe sold a mess of cattle. That's not a crime. What we need is something that will prove he sold more cattle through Lawton than he actually owned or had a legal right to sell."

Wray thought that over and then nodded. "Like the ranch's tally book," he suggested.

"Exactly," Travis said, and his eyes flashed at the idea. "If we could get our hands on that, it would wrap up the case against McCabe. Then I think Judge Shaw would have to agree that there's reason to issue a stay of execution while the partnership between McCabe and Yates is investigated further.''

He was pinning his hopes on the judge being reasonable, Travis knew, but it was the one chance they had to stop the hanging. He had been unable to find anything that negated the evidence against Ruth. The only alternative open to him was to point out that someone else could have had a motive to murder Yates, creating what he hoped was a reasonable doubt.

It was a long shot, but Travis had to take it. If Wray and he could get McCabe's tally book, it would help make a stronger case.

They stopped at one of Laramie's general stores on their way out of town to pick up more supplies. With the added stop at the Trident ranch, Travis knew they would have to ride without stopping, except for short breaks to rest the horses, in order to reach Cheyenne in time. Once they arrived at the ranch, Travis would stay out of sight while Wray slipped into the ranch house and got the tally book. The young cowboy knew his way around the place and was confident he could locate the book and get out without being spotted. Travis and Wray hashed over this plan as they rode out of Laramie, past the maze of big cattle pens on the edge of town.

As he rode, Travis was lost in thought, and he almost did not notice the four men who came around the corner of one of the pens on horseback.

Then he suddenly stiffened, his senses shouting a warning, and Wray did the same beside him. Thirty yards or so in front of them, the four riders had halted abruptly. Travis recognized the dark, surly face of Doak Lawton as the hardcase stared at them in surprise.

"It's that goddamn marshal!" Lawton yelled to his men. His hand flashed toward his gun.

Travis let his instincts take over. He jerked his horse's head to the left and spurred it into motion. The animal leapt to the side as Travis palmed out his Colt. He heard the boom of Lawton's pistol and saw the puff of flame and smoke from its muzzle.

Wray veered to the right so that Lawton and his men would have to split their fire. He jerked out his gun and triggered off a quick shot as he leaned over the neck of his horse.

Travis rode hard into a gap between two of the pens. The corrals were full of cattle, and the beasts began to bawl and mill around nervously as more shots rang out. The men with Lawton were spurring after their quarry and firing, too.

Bullets whined through the air above the horns of the cattle. Men who had been working in the stockyards scurried for cover as the battle broke out. Travis wheeled his horse around another corner. Dust was billowing up from the hooves of the galloping horses and trampling cattle, making it hard to see. Travis held his fire, unwilling to waste bullets on unseen targets. He heard the flat whine of a slug passing close to his head.

Joel Wray headed for the line of trees that marked the banks of the Laramie River. He glanced over his shoulder and saw that one of Lawton's men was riding hard after him. Beyond the pursuer, Wray saw the clouds of dust in the cattle yard and knew that somewhere inside it Luke Travis was fighting for his life against Lawton and the other two men. Pistols banged and cracked in the obscuring clouds.

Wray's horse was rested, but the outlaw's mount

had more speed. The young cowboy grimaced as he realized he would not reach the trees in time. The man pursuing him was almost in pistol range already, and there was no cover between the cattle pens and the river.

Hauling back savagely on the reins, Wray pulled his horse around in a sliding turn that raised some dust. He was facing Lawton's man now. The man gaped in surprise and pulled on his reins when Wray spurred his horse and charged. The outlaw had clearly not expected Wray to go on the offensive. He jerked his gun up and started firing.

What felt like a white-hot poker ripped through Wray's sleeve and ran a fiery path up his left arm. He grunted in pain and swayed in the saddle, but he clamped the hand of the injured arm on the saddle horn and braced himself as his horse pounded ahead. He lifted his gun and squeezed the trigger twice, the pistol blasting and bucking back against his palm.

Lawton's man spun crazily off the back of his horse. His gun slipped from suddenly nerveless fingers and thudded to the dust an instant after its owner landed heavily. The outlaw rolled, tumbled, and finally came to rest in a motionless sprawl.

Wincing from the pain in his bullet-creased arm, Wray holstered his gun and then gathered the reins in his right hand. He slowed the horse from a gallop and walked the animal over to check the man he had shot. The hardcase was lying on his back, his arms and legs splayed out. Blood gushed from the wound in his chest. It had been a lucky shot, Wray reflected grimly, but it had done the job.

Gunfire crackling from the cattle pens reminded him that Luke Travis was still in plenty of trouble.

Wray wheeled his horse around and galloped toward the corrals.

Inside the maze of pens, nightmarish noise assaulted Travis's ears. Gunshots, angry yells, and the bawling of terrified cattle blended together to make it hard to think, let alone keep track of where Lawton and his men were. Travis squinted against the stinging dust and kept moving. If he stopped, Lawton and the others would pin him down.

As Travis rounded one of the pens, a shape suddenly loomed out of the billowing dust only a few feet away. The marshal heard a guttural curse, then was almost deafened by the blast of a revolver. The bullet sizzled by his ear, and he snapped a return shot. The other man jerked and slid to the side, firing again as he fell off his horse. This bullet smacked harmlessly into the ground. The man rolled over and came up on his knees. Clutching at his body with his free hand, he tried to lift his gun to fire a final shot.

Travis yanked his horse around and galloped into the dust cloud. The wounded man pitched forward onto his face, the final shot unfired.

For a fleeting second, Travis wondered if Wray was all right. He had last seen the cowboy heading toward the river with an outlaw in pursuit. Wray was a tough young man, but he might not be a match for one of Lawton's ruthless killers.

A shot cracked behind him, snapping him out of his concern about Wray. He ducked instinctively, and the slug whistled over his head. Turning in the saddle, he saw one of Lawton's men galloping down an alley toward him. Travis urged his horse forward, then jerked it around another corner.

The turn was too much for the frightened horse. It

lost its balance, and Travis barely had time to kick his feet free of the stirrups as it fell. He landed hard on his left shoulder and tumbled over. The outlaw was almost on top of him, riding hard and bent on trampling him.

Travis flung himself to the side, rolling desperately. Hooves pounded the dirt inches from his head. He wound up on his stomach as the man tried to stop his horse and turn the animal for another try.

The dust cleared for a second, long enough for Travis to see the man struggling with his horse. The outlaw pointed his gun at Travis and snapped a shot that kicked up dirt a foot away.

The marshal summoned up all the iron nerve he had developed during his years as a lawman. Coolly, he lifted his gun and fired from his prone position. The upward-angling bullet caught Lawton's man in the chest. He swayed, then tumbled from the saddle as his horse bolted.

Travis had no time to congratulate himself on his marksmanship. Someone howled a curse behind him. The marshal surged to his feet and spun around in time to see Doak Lawton, his dark face contorted in rage, charging toward him on horseback.

Travis glanced around for his horse. The mare was nowhere to be seen. It must have gotten to its feet after the fall and run away from the dust and chaos. Travis was in a narrow alley, barely ten feet wide, between pens. He had no place to hide from Lawton's attack. He would have to meet it head-on.

Lawton's pistol blasted. Travis lifted his Colt and tried to sight in on the rustler through the swirling dust. Suddenly more hoofbeats thundered behind him, but he could not turn his attention from

Lawton's immediate threat. Lawton's second bullet tugged at his sleeve.

Joel Wray rode through the dust cloud. The cowboy hurtled off the back of his horse and landed beside Luke Travis, gun in hand. Travis and Wray fired simultaneously, the twin blasts of their Colts almost indistinguishable. Both slugs crashed into Doak Lawton's chest, and the outlaw flew out of his saddle. He thudded lifelessly to the ground.

Travis and Wray stood silently watching Lawton for any sign of life. Then Travis sighed and slid his Colt into its holster. "Thanks," he breathed to Wray.

"Glad I got here in time to pitch in," Wray said. "I hope you didn't think I was running out on you."

"I figured you'd be back once you'd taken care of that other fella," Travis replied. "We'd better find my horse. This little fracas has slowed us down some."

Wray nodded, then grabbed his horse's reins and mounted. Looking down at Travis, he said, "Lawton called you marshal. How did he know that?"

"McCabe knew," Travis said bleakly. "Lawton must have talked to him in the last couple of days. I don't think Lawton and his men followed us up here, though. Running into them was pure bad luck."

"You're damn right it was, mister," a new voice said. Travis and Wray turned to see several men striding toward them. The one who had spoken had a rifle trained on them, and a sheriff's star was pinned to his vest. "You boys just stand still," he went on. "I want to know how come you went and fought a war in my town."

Chapter Fourteen

❧

BY THURSDAY MORNING PENELOPE YATES WAS SO CON-
sumed by doubts about her father's business dealings
that she was unable to think of anything else. Ever
since Simon Smith and Joel Wray had visited her two
nights earlier, she had asked herself if her father could
have been mixed up in something unlawful, but she
could not bring herself to believe it.

As she thought about the partnership, she decided
she could definitely see Flint McCabe in such a role.
She recalled that during her childhood she sensed how
ambitious he was, although she thought nothing of the
trait at the time. Somehow, because he was her
father's partner, it was acceptable. But now she wondered if that driving ambition had led him to engage
in illegal activities. If so, she could easily imagine his
being part of a rustling ring.

After breakfast Thursday morning, she went to the

desk and took the documents Simon had given her from the locked drawer. She spread the pages out and studied them for several long minutes, but no matter how hard she tried to find her father's innocence in the numbers, the results were the same.

And despite the words that Joel Wray had spoken to reassure her, she did not believe for an instant that Flint McCabe could have been behind the rustling by himself. For one thing, these records were in her father's handwriting. For another, she knew quite well that Roland T. Yates had always been fully aware of everything that went on in his business enterprises.

Her father had known about it, all right. Everything she possessed, she realized, could have come from tainted money. That thought prompted her to gaze around at the luxurious furnishings in the parlor and feel uncomfortable. And as that realization came over Penny, she knew what she had to do.

No one must ever know that her father had been a criminal. She would shield his memory, even if she had not been able to protect him from death. And she was certain she could convince Joel Wray to keep silent, too.

She gathered up the papers, retied the string around them, and went to the huge fireplace with its massive mantel. Now that it was summer, the fireplace was cold; it had not been lit since before her father's death. Placing the bundle on the mantel, Penny bent down and carefully reached up into the chimney, trying not to get soot on the sleeve of her dress.

It had been years since she had done this, but it came back to her in a rush. Her searching fingers ran over the inside wall of the chimney until they touched the loose brick. Working it back and forth for a few minutes, she was able to pull it free. Behind the brick was a small space where she had hidden things as a child. Now, after all this time, she could not remember what she had once put there. But the niche was empty and would be just big enough for the documents.

Holding the loose brick, she withdrew her hand and winced at the soot on her dress. The oily black dirt had fallen on her arm when she pulled the brick out. She had to do something about the dress so no one would know where she had hidden the records. She hoped the dress could be cleaned—but even if it was permanently soiled and therefore ruined, the loss would be worthwhile.

She took the bundle off the mantel and stuffed it into the hiding place. After she had replaced the brick, Penny went upstairs, changed into a clean dress, and carried the soiled garment back down to give to the maid to clean.

As she reached the bottom of the stairs, someone knocked on the front door. She was only a few steps away, so she decided to answer the knock herself. Carefully tucking the soiled sleeve inside, she folded the dress and placed it on a table in the hall. When she swung the door open, she saw Flint McCabe standing on the veranda, holding his hat.

"Good morning, Penny," he said, smiling.

"Hello, Flint," she said coolly. She could not keep the icy edge from her tone now that she knew about McCabe and his activities.

"You don't sound too happy to see me."

Penny shook her head. "I'm sorry, I'm just not feeling too well this morning."

"Maybe I can cheer you up." McCabe gestured with his hat and raised his eyebrows. "Can I come in?"

"Of course." Penny stepped back to allow him to enter. McCabe strolled past her into the parlor and sat down in an overstuffed armchair, making himself at home.

Penny sat at the end of the sofa, as far away from him as she could get. She did not attempt to be gracious or offer him anything, but instead asked bluntly, "Are you here for a reason, Flint?"

McCabe leaned forward, placed his hands on his knees, and regarded her earnestly. "I sure am, Penny," he said. "I know how you've been feeling ever since . . . well, ever since your father died. You've got a right to mourn, of course, but I hate to see you pining away like this. I think it's time we did something to snap you out of it."

The oily smoothness of his words fanned the hatred in Penny. She now despised his arrogance and his utter confidence in himself. McCabe had been the one to suggest the rustling scheme, she was sure of that. And her father had been too weak to oppose it. That was a bitter pill for Penny to swallow, but she believed it was the truth.

She tried to control her temper as she said, "Just what is it you propose to do, Flint?"

He grinned. "'Propose.' Now, that's an interesting choice of words. You know how I feel about you, Penny, how I've felt for a couple of years now. Roland always hoped that you and I would wind up together. I think it's time we made his dream come true."

"You mean . . . you want me to marry you? Now?"

McCabe shook his head. "It would hardly be proper

right now, what with Roland's death being so recent. But I think we could go ahead and make it official, announce our engagement and all. And then in six months or so, I'll throw the biggest wedding party this territory's ever seen." He stood up and came over to the sofa, sinking into its cushions close beside her. He reached out and grasped her hand. "How about it, Penny?" he asked.

"No!" she shrieked, unable to control her feelings any longer. Repelled by his touch, she jerked her hand from his and cringed back against the sofa. "I could never marry you after what you did to my father . . . turning him into a criminal . . . !" The accusation tumbled from her lips.

McCabe's face hardened. "What the devil are you talking about?" he demanded impatiently.

Furious, Penny said without thinking, "I saw those papers of my father's! I know about the rustling and how you were using the money to buy land. I know all about it, Flint, and I hate you for getting him mixed up in it!"

McCabe's handsome face looked as if it were carved out of stone. "I don't know what the hell you're talking about," he snapped.

But his eyes told a different story. In them, Penny could see that her accusations were true. She saw something else, too. She started to stand up.

McCabe's hand shot out and clasped her wrist. Roughly he pulled her back onto the sofa, then pinned her down with one strong arm.

"Let . . . let me up!" she gasped.

"Not until you tell me what you're talking about," McCabe said. "Has someone been spreading lies about me?"

"They're not lies! My father kept records of all those transactions."

"And where are these documents?" McCabe hissed.

"I—I don't have them anymore," Penny stammered.

McCabe lifted his other hand and savagely slapped her face. She cried out, and tears welled in her eyes.

"You'd better tell me the truth," he grated. "I don't have time to waste on you, Penny."

"I told you," she said, fighting back her tears. "I don't have them."

"You're lying." McCabe stood up, dragging her with him. "But I'll make you tell me the truth."

There was a quick patter of hurrying footsteps in the hall. The maid appeared in the parlor doorway. With an anxious look on her face, she said, "I heard you cry out, miss. Are you all right?"

McCabe swung around to face the young woman while he fiercely gripped Penny's wrist. Smiling, he said, "Miss Yates is just overwrought right now. Isn't that right, Penny?"

The pain and pressure on Penny's wrist made her want to scream, but she knew McCabe would do more to hurt her if she did not go along with him. "Y-yes," she stammered. "I was just . . . thinking about my father. . . ."

"I think you need a ride, Penny," McCabe declared. "That'll clear your head. I've got my wagon right outside. How about it?" The steely determination in his voice was as strong as the grip that encircled her wrist.

Penny nodded jerkily. "Yes. That . . . that sounds fine."

McCabe picked up his hat with his free hand and

put it on. "Come along, then. You won't need a wrap; it's a lovely day."

Putting his arm around her shoulders, McCabe steered Penny from the parlor. She glanced nervously at the folded dress on the table and prayed he would not notice it. Repressing another urge to cry for help, she let him lead her out of the house and down the walk to the buckboard that was tethered to the fence outside the gate.

"Climb up," McCabe ordered once they reached the wagon. Penny did as she was told. The rancher jerked the reins free from the fence, then climbed onto the seat beside her. As he flicked the lines and got the horses moving, he went on. "You don't have to be afraid of me, Penny. I'm sorry if I hurt you back there. I just wanted to get us out where we could talk without being disturbed."

"I don't have anything to say to you." Penny's voice was little more than a whisper.

"Oh, I think you do." McCabe turned the wagon around a corner. He had the team moving at a fairly good clip, handling the animals with practiced ease. "I want to know about those records you mentioned."

"There aren't any," Penny ventured. "I . . . I just made the whole thing up."

McCabe shook his head without looking at her. "I'm sorry, my dear, but I just don't believe you. You see, I *know* your father kept records of what we were doing. I always advised him not to, but you know how he was. He liked to have everything down in black and white." McCabe snorted contemptuously. "Well, it certainly backfired on him, and on me, too. But if you've got those papers now, I want them."

Penny tried to force her brain to work. Something in McCabe's statement struck her as strange, but she was too upset and frightened to figure out what it was. She saw the glances of the townspeople they passed in the buckboard and wanted to call out for help, but she knew it would do no good. Flint McCabe would just spin some more of his smooth lies. No one would believe her if she accused him of being a rustler and a kidnapper.

But kidnapping her was exactly what he was doing. He knew now that she had seen the documents and understood what they meant. He could not afford to let her tell anyone.

God, did he intend to kill her? Penny would not put it past him. She had seen the look in his eyes and knew he would do anything he thought necessary to protect himself.

As she blinked back her tears, she realized those documents were the only leverage she had. The buckboard was passing through the edge of town, heading north to the trail that led to Trident. He was going to take her to the ranch, she thought. Once there, he would feel he could do anything he wanted to her.

He had been silent for several minutes, but now, as they moved from the outskirts of Cheyenne into the open range, he coaxed, "You and I have been friends for a long time, Penny, ever since you were a girl. I don't want us to become enemies now. Just tell me where those papers are, so I can get them and dispose of them. Once that's done, nothing else has to change between us."

His voice was soft and persuasive, and Penny knew he was trying to charm her. Over the years she had heard stories about all the women who had been in love with the dashing Flint McCabe. She knew he was accustomed to getting whatever he wanted. But she could easily resist; this time he was up against some-one who had every reason to hate him.

"I saw the papers," she said abruptly. "I know what they mean. But they're in a safe place where you'll never get your hands on them. If anything happens to me, they'll go to the authorities."

She knew her threat was hollow, but it was the best she could manage. She just hoped it was convincing enough to make McCabe hesitate before he tried anything extreme.

He did not reply for a long moment, concentrating instead on driving the team of horses. "What do you intend to do with the documents?" he asked at last.

Penny took a deep breath, then told him the truth. "I planned to see to it that no one ever found out about them."

"You don't want your father's memory dishonored, is that it?" McCabe nodded thoughtfully. "That's probably wise, Penny."

"Then you'll turn around and take me back home?" she asked.

McCabe shook his head. "Not with the way you feel about me now. I know you, Penny. You're going to want to get even with me. Sooner or later, you'll want to settle the score for what you think I've done, both today and in the past. I can't allow that."

"So what are you going to do?"

He grinned. "Just like I said. I'm going to marry you—right away."

Sick fear churned in Penny's stomach. She could

not stand the thought of being married to this man. He was evil, and besides, she loved Joel Wray. There had to be some way out of this! "I . . . I can't marry—" she began.

"Of course you can, and you will!" McCabe snapped. "You see, Penny, there's a law that says a court can't force a wife to testify against her husband. Once we're married, nobody can make you say anything you shouldn't, and I won't have to worry, will I?"

Penny knew what he said was true, but she also knew a woman could voluntarily testify against her husband. But if she did, she would expose her father.

Turning to look at him, Penny shook her head, but she could tell from the cold, knowing smile he gave her that he did not believe her for an instant. After they were married and he owned her share of the partnership, he would take steps to ensure that she would not talk.

Penny fell silent, and McCabe did not seem to have anything more to say. The wagon rolled on toward the ranch. As she watched the passing country she realized they would be there in a little over an hour, and Penny wondered if she would ever again see Cheyenne and her home.

About half an hour later, Penny spoke. "Could you stop for a minute, Flint?" she asked softly.

"What for?"

"So that I can walk around for a bit. You have to remember, I'm not used to riding in a buckboard for this long."

McCabe considered for a moment, then nodded. "I guess these plank seats are pretty hard, all right." He pointed at some trees to the left and swung the wagon. "There's a nice little creek over there. We'll stop in the shade."

A few moments later he drew the wagon to a stop beneath one of the trees that lined the creek. Through the underbrush Penny could see the stream; the sunlight was glittering prettily on the water. It was cool in the shade, and the creek bubbled musically. It would have been a very pleasant spot—if Joel Wray had been beside her on the seat, and not Flint McCabe.

"I'm glad you decided to be reasonable about this, Penny," McCabe said as he climbed down from the wagon and came around to assist her. "There's no reason you and I have to be enemies, no reason at all."

"Of course not, Flint. Thank you."

She caught him watching her warily, being cautious in case she tried to trick him. But as they strolled side by side along the creek bank, she felt him begin to relax.

The brush thinned out so that Penny could stand on the edge of the bank and look across the creek. She calculated it was about a dozen feet wide and three or four feet deep with a steady, gentle current.

As she stood there, McCabe moved behind her and placed his hands on her shoulders. In a husky voice, he said, "For years now, I've thought you were the loveliest woman I've ever seen, Penny. I've been biding my time, building up the ranch so that one day you could be the mistress of the biggest spread in the territory."

"You did . . . all of those things . . . for me?" she stammered.

"The rustling? Sure. Oh, I'll admit I enjoy the money and the power, and so did your father. But both of us wanted the best for you, Penny."

A spasm of revulsion passed through her, but McCabe evidently mistook it for another emotion. He pulled her against him, started turning her to face him.

Penny abruptly twisted in his arms. Her hand shot toward his face, her long fingernails stabbing at his eyes and raking down his cheek. McCabe let out a yell as Penny clawed him. She grabbed his jacket and kept turning, spinning them both around on the edge of the bank. She meant to push him into the water if she could, but suddenly the earth crumbled beneath her. She felt herself falling.

McCabe fell with her. They landed with a huge splash. Under the water, Penny tore herself from his grip and then surfaced, gasping for air. Fighting the weight of her sodden gown, she struggled to the muddy bank and started to scramble up it. Her frenzied brain told her that if she could get to the wagon before him, she could escape, leaving him here. Excitement surged through her as she reached the top of the bank. She would get the documents from the chimney and go to Sheriff Dehner with them! It was too late to protect her father's name now, but she could make sure that McCabe was punished for his part in the scheme.

McCabe's fingers clamped around her ankle, jerking her foot out from under her and spilling her on the grassy bank. He threw himself on top of her and, as she flailed hysterically at him, grabbed her wrists with one hand. His other fist cracked against her jaw, knocking her head to the side. Shocked by his violence, Penny stopped fighting. She lay in the grass, panting heavily and staring up at McCabe.

"Goddamn bitch!" he snapped. He let go of her and got quickly to his feet. As he stepped back, he pulled the gun from his holster and cocked the hammer. He grated, "I don't know if these cartridges will fire after that little swim, but I guarantee that if you try anything else, we'll sure as hell find out!"

Penny stayed where she was, sprawled on the ground and silent except for her heaving gasps.

After a moment McCabe bent down, grasped her arm, and pulled her to her feet. He shoved her toward the wagon. "Get up there!" he ordered. "I see now I can't trust you, Penny, so we'll just do things my way from now on."

Stunned by all that had happened, she climbed numbly onto the wagon seat. It was too much, coming as it did on top of everything else that had occurred recently. She did nothing and was quiet as McCabe stepped up and sat down next to her. He transferred the gun to his left hand and picked up the reins with his right. Glaring at her, he flapped the reins and clucked to the team to get them moving toward Trident again.

Neither one spoke for the rest of the trip. Penny's clothes were soaked, but the chill that gripped her did not come from the wet garments. While the warm sunshine soon dried her dress, she was still cold inside. She always would be, she thought, as long as she was in Flint McCabe's hands.

As they approached the two-story whitewashed ranch house, McCabe finally holstered his gun. If the cowhands who were working in the corrals nearby thought anything of their boss driving in with the lovely blonde, both of them with their hair and clothes in disarray, they said nothing. With a hand clasped firmly around her upper arm, McCabe led Penny into the big ranch house.

She had visited Trident many times before, had always thought it was a lovely house with its veranda that wrapped around three sides, cozily nestled in a grove of trees. The heavy, comfortable furniture inside was expensive but very different from the ornate, elegant furnishings of her own home. Trident was a man's preserve that she once found pleasant. But now she saw it as an evil place.

McCabe pulled her into the big parlor, led her to a chair, and roughly shoved her into it. "You just sit there for a while," he growled.

Penny finally found her voice. "What are you going to do with me?" she whispered.

"I told you what I'm going to do. I'm going to marry you, dammit."

"I can still testify of my own free will, even if I'm married to you." She knew her words might well seal her death warrant, but she did not want him to think that she was going to cooperate meekly.

McCabe shook his head. "You won't be going anywhere to testify to anything. You're going to stay here on this ranch, right in this house." He grinned, and it was an ugly expression. "A husband's got a right to keep his wife at home, doesn't he?"

He turned away and called sharply to someone with an odd-sounding name. A moment later, a Chinese man wearing an apron appeared in the parlor doorway. "Go find a couple of the boys and send them in here," McCabe instructed the cook. "I've got a chore for them. They're going to be standing guard over something that's mighty valuable to me."

Penny knew what he meant. She was a prisoner, and if McCabe had his way, she would remain so from now on.

"I'll send someone into town for your things," he said, turning back to her. "You tell me where those papers are, and I'll get them, too."

Penny shook her head.

McCabe shrugged. "Have it your way. You'll tell me sooner or later, or I'll tear that house apart until I find them. Either way, I'll get them, and then nobody will ever give orders to Flint McCabe again, by God!"

Again there was something strange about his words, but her stunned brain refused to comprehend. She stared silently at the Navajo rug on the floor, until McCabe finally cursed bitterly and stomped out of the room. Vaguely, she heard booted feet on the veranda, heard his voice issue orders to the cowboys the cook had brought, giving them instructions to watch her.

This was just the first day, she thought. The first day of a prison sentence that could last the rest of her life.

Chapter Fifteen

LUKE TRAVIS AND JOEL WRAY SPENT AN HOUR IN THE
Laramie sheriff's office, trying to convince the local
lawman that they were not gun-crazy outlaws. Travis
produced his marshal's badge, and several cattle-yard
workers who had witnessed the uproar testified that
Lawton and his men had started the fight. Still angry
that a gun battle had been waged in his town, the
sheriff finally agreed that Travis and Wray had not
been at fault.

"You'll have to stay for the inquest," the local
lawman growled as he returned their guns to them.

As Travis strapped his holster to his hip, he glanced
at the clock on the wall and saw that it was already
past noon. Looking at Wray, he nodded toward the
door. "Sorry, Sheriff," he said, shaking his head
slowly. "We can't do that. You've got our statements.
They'll have to do."

The sheriff's face reddened. "Say, you don't come in here and give me orders—"

"I'm not," Travis cut in coldly. "I'm just telling you that we're leaving. We've got to be back in Cheyenne by nine o'clock tomorrow morning, and that's going to take some hard riding."

The sheriff regarded the two grim-faced men for a long moment, then sighed. "All right, get the hell out of here," he snapped. "I don't want to see you in Laramie again, you understand?"

"I don't think you have to worry about that, Sheriff," Wray replied.

Travis had already turned and was heading for the door.

Three minutes later they were on their horses, traveling east toward the edge of town. As they passed the cattle pens, Travis glanced at the scene of the shoot-out. The bodies of Lawton and his men had been removed. The cattle were calm again, and the choking clouds of dust had settled. No evidence remained of the desperate battle that had been fought there only a little over an hour before.

As they left Laramie behind, Travis urged his horse into a fast trot. He needed every ounce of speed the animal could give without killing it, but in the end, if it took riding the mare into the ground, he would do it.

It was going to be a long afternoon and a longer night. But probably not long enough, Travis thought bleakly.

They ate in the saddle and, when night fell, took turns dozing as they rode. The weather stayed clear, so once again the moon and stars shone brightly enough to show them the road. Travis lost track of time, and his exhaustion numbed him to everything but the sound of galloping hooves and the motion of the saddle beneath him.

An hour before dawn, as the sky in the east was beginning to lighten, Joel Wray pointed to the southeast. "We'll angle off the road here and head for Trident," he said.

Travis was thankful that the young cowboy was with him. He doubted that he could have found the ranch by himself. Uncapping his canteen, he drank deeply, then splashed some of the water on his face. He shook his head to clear away the sleepiness.

Trying to stifle a yawn, he slipped his watch from his pocket and opened it. The moon was setting now, but, coupled with the brightening sky, it cast enough light for him to read the watch face. A little after five o'clock. If they could get away from Trident around six, even allowing for a slower pace from their exhausted horses, they would reach Cheyenne sometime before eight—plenty of time to stop the hanging.

They were going to make it. The thought sent a surge of adrenaline coursing through him, driving away the rest of his weariness. Because of this night of hard riding, they would get back in time.

If nothing else slowed them down, he reminded himself grimly. They still had to get that tally book.

They rode for another half hour, Wray leading the way across the rolling range. The eastern horizon was starting to turn pink with the approaching sunrise when Wray pulled his horse to a stop. The animal's head drooped with fatigue, as did Travis's when the marshal halted beside him.

"The ranch is down there about a mile," Wray said,

gesturing into the valley that spread below them from their vantage point on the top of a ridge.

Travis followed Wray's outstretched arm and saw pinpoints of light burning. "Somebody's already up," he commented.

"That's not unusual. McCabe expects his men to work hard, and that means hitting the saddle at daybreak. The men eat their chow in the bunkhouse, and I figure McCabe'll be with the men giving them their orders for the day. There shouldn't be anybody in the main house when I slip in."

"Won't folks be wondering where you are?"

Wray grinned. "I imagine they've already decided that I just up and pulled out. Payday was last week, so I only had a few day's wages coming, not enough to matter to a light-footed cowboy."

"You'd better be careful anyway. McCabe doesn't know you're working against him, but he still might try to gun you if he catches you inside the house."

Wray gave a short, humorless laugh. "Trading shots with McCabe might not be so bad."

"The two of you blasting each other won't help my sister-in-law," Travis pointed out. "I need that tally book, Joel."

"You'll get it," Wray assured him. He urged his horse into a walk. "Come on. We can get a little closer before I move in on my own."

Penny had slept very little, despite the soft bed in the room that McCabe had taken her to the night before. She was afraid he would try to have his way with her, but he had been a gentleman. She had been sullen and silent, but that did not seem to shake

McCabe's faith that sooner or later he would win her over.

And if he did not, well, then he would just keep her a prisoner here in this house for the rest of her life—or until he got tired of having her around. If that happened, Penny knew, he would silence her permanently.

Yesterday as soon as McCabe had positioned his men around the house, he disappeared to attend to ranch business. Penny stayed in the parlor for the rest of the day, sometimes pacing up and down the large room, sometimes giving in to fatigue brought on by frustration and despair and dozing on the sofa.

Several times during the afternoon, McCabe returned and asked her about the records that her father had kept, but Penny did not answer him. The rancher only shrugged and left. She realized he could afford to be patient now that she was in his power. He had sent word into town to her servants, telling them that she had decided to stay at the ranch for a while. They were to close up the house and leave for the time being. No one would miss her, she knew; no one would come to her aid.

That evening after a strained, silent supper with him in the large dining room, McCabe had taken her to the small spare bedroom. When she finally lay down on the bed, she kept her dress on. McCabe had given her an elegant nightgown that came all the way from St. Louis, he said, but Penny knew that she would have felt uncomfortable wearing it, as if that would somehow represent a victory for McCabe. For long hours, she tossed and turned and stared at the ceiling of the second-floor bedroom. Visions of

McCabe being suitably punished for his crimes filled her thoughts. She wondered if that man Travis could have been right. She no longer doubted that McCabe could have been responsible for her father's death.

Finally, sometime in the dark hours of the night, she dozed.

When she awoke, the sky outside the window of her room was gray with approaching light. She was groggy, and her head hurt. Her dress had a strange odor, due no doubt to the dunking in the creek.

She went to the door of the room and paused there, listening. She heard a soft snore right outside; that would be her guard, napping on duty. The door itself had been locked, and the room's single window was nailed shut. She had checked that right away, then given up any thoughts of escape. Breaking out would make enough racket to summon the guard, even if the man was sleeping on the job.

Penny's mouth was achingly dry, and she had other needs that required attention. She knocked on the door, rapping sharply enough to awaken the guard outside. She heard the thump as his chair legs hit the floor, then a moment later he grunted, "What you want, lady?"

"I . . . I need to use the outhouse," Penny replied, almost overcome with embarrassment. She wished that McCabe had had the foresight to have a chamber pot put in the room.

"Sure, sure," the guard said. "Let me find the key."

A few seconds later, Penny heard the key rattle in the lock. The man swung the door open and stepped back to let her come into the hall. He was a young, bearded cowhand. She did not remember seeing him before on any of her trips to the ranch, but that meant nothing. Cowboys came and went all the time. At least he was not leering at her, and she was thankful for that much. He watched her with sleepy eyes as she went down the hall toward the rear stairs.

"Reckon you know your way around the place," he commented, "you bein' the late mayor's daughter an' all."

"That's right," Penny replied. "I don't appreciate being treated like this, either."

The cowboy shrugged, and the barrel of the rifle in his arms bobbed up and down. "Ain't none of my affair. I reckon the boss has got his reasons for what he's doin'."

"He has a reason, all right," Penny snapped. "He's a cruel man who's trying to save his own skin."

"Wouldn't know nothin' about that, ma'am. Say, once you're done, I imagine Cookie's got some break-fast ready if'n you're hungry. I could do with a mite to eat myself."

Penny made no reply. The guard took her outside in the dawn light and stood a respectable distance away while she made use of the outhouse. Then he followed her as she went back to the main building. Penny glanced around, wondering if it would be possible to make a dash for freedom. Surely McCabe had not instructed his men to shoot her if she tried to escape.

But then she thought about it and decided that the risk was too great. Her guard had treated her decently so far, but she was not willing to risk her life on his crude chivalry.

When Luke Travis and Joel Wray were within a few hundred yards of the ranch house, they reined in. The young cowboy left Travis waiting on the far side of a brushy rise and continued toward the house. As he circled wide around the bunkhouse, he saw a few men moving around the building. Others were at the corral, saddling their horses for the day's work. Keeping an eye on them, Wray stayed in the trees and brush as much as he could and continued to circle until he had put the main house between the bunkhouse and him.

Wray eased out of the saddle and tied his horse to a sapling. From here he would go on foot. He paused to check the loads in his Colt, then slipped the gun back in its holster. Despite what he had said about welcoming a gun duel with McCabe, he knew that he had to be careful. There would be time to face down McCabe later, after Ruth Carson's execution had been postponed.

The house loomed before him. A veranda ran around the front and both sides of the house, and several doors opened onto it. He headed for the side door closest to him. His boots seemed to thump loudly on the planks of the porch as he stepped across it, but he knew that was just his nerves. He was moving as silently as he could.

Wray slowly inched the screen door toward him to prevent the hinges from squeaking. When he had it open, he tried the knob of the wooden door. It turned freely, as he thought it would. Nobody locked doors around here, not even skunks like McCabe. The crooked rancher was probably convinced he had nothing to worry about.

Pausing just inside the door, Wray listened intently. He did not hear any voices or footsteps. The Chinese cook was probably at the bunkhouse serving breakfast. McCabe should be over with the hands, giving them their chores for the day, just as he had told Travis. Wray was betting that he had the house to himself.

Although enough daylight was filtering into the house to allow him to make his way around, many of the rooms were still shadowy. McCabe's office was located in a rear corner of the house; Wray had always picked up his pay there and was familiar with it. He slipped through a couple of sitting rooms and down a long hall to the door of the office. This one was not locked, either, and he breathed a sigh of relief once he was inside and had closed the door behind him.

Hurrying to the big desk that stood against one wall, Wray started pawing through the litter of papers on its top. He had seen the tally book several times, knew that McCabe used a small, leather-covered ledger for that purpose. It was not on top of the desk, so Wray had no choice but to start going through the drawers. He opened them carefully, again trying not to make any noise.

In the second drawer he tried, his fingers brushed against a leather binding. He pulled the book from a stack of papers and thought it looked like the right one. To be sure, he flipped through its pages, squinting in the dim light to make out the writing, and he smiled when he saw he had found what he was looking for.

He closed the book, slipped it under his shirt, and turned to leave. He had taken one step toward the office door when it suddenly opened.

Flint McCabe stopped in his tracks and stood just inside the doorway, a surprised look on his face. His hand had gone instinctively to the gun on his hip when he saw that there was an intruder in his office, but he stopped before drawing the weapon.

It took every ounce of Wray's self-control not to reach for his Colt. His brain was racing, trying to find a way out of this that would not involve shooting, and as McCabe frowned in recognition, Wray decided on his course of action.

"Is that you, Wray?" McCabe demanded. "What the hell are you doing in here? The foreman told me he thought you'd drifted."

Wray took a deep breath. "I'm planning to," he said. "That's why I'm here, Mr. McCabe. I was looking for you. I want to draw my pay and ride on."

McCabe visibly relaxed. He strode past Wray toward the desk. Wray hoped he did not notice that someone had been going through his papers. The desk had been in enough of a mess to start with that there was a good chance McCabe would not notice that anything had been disturbed.

"What's the matter, Wray?" McCabe asked. "Haven't you been happy here?"

Wray did not turn all the way around to face McCabe. He was all too aware of the tally book bulging against his shirt. McCabe had not noticed it yet, and Wray did not want to give him an opportunity to. "Everything's been fine here, boss," he lied. "I reckon I just need to move on. You know how us Texans are."

"Sure," McCabe grunted. He sounded convinced, but his eyes were still narrowed suspiciously.

Wray wanted to leap across the room and smash a fist into his face, but he kept a tight rein on that impulse. Here in McCabe's stronghold, such an action would just get him killed. If he could get away from the ranch and give the tally book to Travis, then he would settle with McCabe later.

The rancher pulled open a desk drawer, and Wray caught his breath when he saw it was the same one in which he had found the tally book. But McCabe just drew out a cash box and opened it, apparently not noticing that the book was gone. He said, "You don't have much pay coming, Wray, just a few days' worth."

"I know," Wray said.

"Why don't you stick around until the end of the month? That'd give me more time to replace you."

"Sorry, Mr. McCabe," Wray said, trying to sound sincere. "I've just got to be riding."

McCabe shrugged. He took a handful of bills and counted out a few. Then he closed the cash box and replaced it in the drawer. Wray held his breath until McCabe had shut the drawer.

The rancher turned and held the money out to Wray. "Here you go," he said. "Before you ride on, why don't you stop at the bunkhouse for some grub? I don't mind feeding you one last meal."

"Thanks," Wray said as he took the bills. He folded them and stuck them in his pants pocket, trying not to look nervous. "I reckon I'd better be heading out, though."

"Suit yourself."

McCabe turned back to the desk, and Wray started toward the door. The cowboy's pulse was hammering in his head. Just a few more minutes, he thought, and he would be safely away from the Trident ranch house. Then it would not matter if McCabe discovered the theft of the tally book.

As Wray touched the doorknob, the door flew open in his face. He stepped back, surprised, his hand going toward his gun. Then he stopped, and his eyes widened in shock as Penny Yates threw herself into his arms and cried, "Joel!"

Wray barely had time to notice the haggard, desperate look on Penny's face before he wrapped his left arm around her and pulled her to him. He saw a ranch hand hurrying after her and recognized him as a man called Daley. Behind Wray, McCabe exclaimed, "What the hell!"

It's all torn now, Wray thought bitterly. McCabe had had no idea there was anything between Penny and him, but the rancher was not blind. He could see it now in the way Penny buried her face against Wray's chest and sobbed.

Wray stepped back quickly, taking Penny with him. With his right hand he drew his gun as McCabe reached for his weapon. Wray said sharply, "Hold it, McCabe! Leave that gun where it is and tell Daley to put his down."

McCabe stopped, his hand frozen a few inches from the butt of his revolver. He stared into the muzzle of Wray's Colt for a long moment, his face flushed with rage. Then he switched his gaze to the obviously confused guard and snapped, "Forget it, Daley! Put the rifle down."

Daley hesitated, then stooped and laid the Winchester on the floor. "Sure, boss. Whatever you say."

Keeping his gun trained on McCabe, Wray asked, "What's going on here, Penny?"

"He . . . he kidnapped me!" Penny stammered in a

choked voice. "He told me that my father and he were partners in that rustling ring, just as you thought, Joel! Oh, God, I thought he was going to kill me. He said he was going to keep me here forever. . . ."

"Take it easy," Wray said grimly. "He's not going to hurt anybody else."

McCabe laughed humorlessly. "Seems to me you've been working both sides, Wray. I thought you rode for me."

"I told you I was quitting, McCabe. I don't work for scum like you."

"You two won't get out of here alive, you know that." McCabe's voice was smugly confident, and he appeared to have gotten over his anger.

"I think we will," Wray declared. "You're going with us to make sure we do."

McCabe slowly shook his head. "I'm not going anywhere. If you want to shoot me, go right ahead. But if you do, Daley there will gun both of you down. You don't want that, do you, Wray?"

Wray hesitated. McCabe was right; if he shot the rancher, he would lose what little leverage he had.

Daley did not give Wray time to make up his mind. He grabbed for the six-gun on his hip, yelling, "I'll get him right now, boss!"

Penny screamed as Wray jerked around and triggered just as Daley's gun cleared leather. The slug slammed into the cowboy's midsection, knocking him back into the hall. Wray whipped around in time to see McCabe lunging toward him. He lashed out with his gun.

The barrel cracked against McCabe's skull. He grunted and staggered past Wray and Penny, his feet tangling and causing him to topple. He fell heavily on the office floor, then shaking his head, he struggled to stand.

Hesitating for only an instant, Wray quickly decided he could not kill the man in cold blood. But he could not give McCabe time to regain his senses, either. Still clutching Penny, he urged, "Come on! We've got to get out of here!"

Half dragging her, he ran from the office toward the side door. That shot would bring McCabe's men on the run, but he believed they had a chance to reach the horse Wray had left hidden in the trees.

Penny was gasping for breath as Wray pulled her onto the porch. He heard booted feet pounding on the veranda, and three Trident cowhands ran around the front corner of the house. Wray snapped a shot over their heads, close enough to make them come to an abrupt stop and duck back around the corner.

Several men rode around the rear corner of the house. They were all holding guns, Wray saw. He had just taken a step toward the edge of the veranda when they opened fire. Bullets chewed up splinters at his feet. Wray dodged back and flattened against the wall of the house, clutching Penny to him. If this kept up, she was liable to catch a stray slug, he thought frantically. There was no way they could get into the trees and reach his horse.

In fact, he thought bitterly, they were good and pinned down, and McCabe would probably push through that side door next to them at any second.

Suddenly Luke Travis galloped toward them through the trees. Guiding his horse with his knees, he led Wray's mount with one hand and fired his pistol with the other. The marshal's accurate fire drove

McCabe's riders back behind the house and forced the men on the front porch to crouch against the wall, but McCabe's men continued to trade shots whenever they had the chance. Travis yelled to Wray, "Come on!"

Wray grinned and plunged recklessly off the porch, his free hand clamped on Penny's arm. He was thankful that Travis had disregarded his suggestion to stay put. The first shot must have brought the man from Kansas on the run, and now they at least had a chance to get away.

Wray jammed his gun into its holster as he reached his horse. Travis had pulled both animals to a stop and was still firing at the front and back corners of the house. Wray reached up, grabbed the saddle horn, and vaulted onto the animal's back. He pulled Penny up, barely feeling her weight, and settled her in front of him in the saddle.

In a hail of bullets from McCabe's men, Travis and he spurred for the safety of the trees. It would be a long run to Cheyenne with McCabe's men dogging their every step, but Wray thought they could make it.

Suddenly Wray's horse stumbled, and the young cowboy realized his animal had been hit. As he felt the horse's legs falter even more, Wray kicked his feet out of the stirrups and gripped Penny tighter. They flew off, just as the wounded animal toppled over on its side. Wray twisted in midair, knowing they were going to hit hard and trying to position himself to land under Penny and take the brunt of the impact. They slammed into the ground, and Wray felt the air whoosh from his lungs.

Wray and Penny tumbled over several times, coming to rest at the foot of a tree. A few yards away, the fallen horse whimpered in agony and then died. Gasping for breath, Wray slapped at his holster, but it was empty. Bleakly he realized his gun had slipped out during the fall. And Penny—

Wray stared at her lifeless form. She lay next to him, her eyes closed, her head lolled back. But then he spotted a strong pulse beating in the clean lines of her throat and knew that she had only been knocked out.

Travis had reined in when Wray's horse was shot out from under him. Wray saw him sitting on his horse nearby and yelled, "Go on, Travis! Get out of here!"

The marshal did not have time to reply. A rifle cracked, the bullet whistling close to Travis's head. From the veranda of the ranch house, Flint McCabe yelled, "Hold it, Travis! I won't miss the next time!"

McCabe held a Winchester, the barrel trained on Travis. Slowly, the marshal sighed and reluctantly dropped his Colt. McCabe's men rode from behind the house to surround the three of them.

"Sorry, Joel," Travis murmured.

"I'm the one who's sorry, Luke," Wray replied as he sat on the ground cradling Penny's head in his lap. "I reckon it was all for nothing. . . ."

"No. You did what you had to do." Travis's voice held no bitterness, no recriminations. But it was too late now to save Ruth. Both of them knew it was just too damned late.

Chapter Sixteen

FLINT MCCABE ORDERED LUKE TRAVIS TO DISMOUNT and walk slowly to the veranda. Then the rancher motioned with his Winchester to Joel Wray to follow the marshal. Wray gently lifted the unconscious Penny and carried her toward the house. Three of McCabe's men came from the porch and walked behind them, training their guns on the two men. Out of the corner of his eye Travis noticed a cowhand scoop up his gun and hunt for Wray's.

When Travis and Wray reached him, McCabe ordered one of his men to open the side door and lead them into the parlor. Once there, Wray eased the unconscious Penny onto the sofa.

The rancher entered the room and grinned triumphantly. "I should have known you were mixed up with Wray somehow, Travis," he said. "You just couldn't leave things alone, could you? And you had to drag Wray into it with you."

"Nobody dragged me into anything," Wray said hotly. "I helped Travis because he's been right about you all along. You're a no-good rustler, McCabe, and I reckon I'm about the only one on this ranch who didn't know it."

"Not the only one," the rancher replied. "But the others who didn't know are miles away at the line shacks. I sent them off yesterday after I brought Penny here. So there's nobody around to help you two." He jerked the barrel of the Winchester and spoke to his men. "A couple of you search them, make sure they don't have any hidden weapons."

Travis and Wray had to stand still while McCabe's men carried out his instructions. A moment later, one of them said, "No guns or knives on them, boss, but look at this!" He held up the tally book, which he had found under Wray's shirt.

McCabe snatched the book from the cowboy's hand. "Dammit!" he exclaimed. "You're bold as brass, aren't you, Wray? You figured you'd get enough evidence on me to send me to prison, didn't you?"

"Or hang you," Wray shot back.

McCabe laughed. "Nobody's going to hang except that Carson woman. Once nine o'clock comes around, this case is going to be closed for good. Nobody's ever going to have a reason to poke in it again. But just for your information, Travis, I didn't kill Yates. Didn't have a damn thing to do with it."

Travis frowned. McCabe sounded sincere, and lying at this point was senseless, now that they were McCabe's prisoners. Besides, the rancher had freely admitted he was behind the rustling, so why would he deny being involved in Yates's murder if it was not true?

But that would mean that Ruth was guilty, and Travis refused to accept that. Unless someone else, someone he had not even considered, had killed the mayor.

"Take them upstairs and lock them up, all three of them," McCabe ordered harshly. "I'll let you live until nine o'clock, Travis. That seems appropriate. Then I'll dispose of you and Wray."

"What about Penny?" Wray asked, his face grim.

McCabe leered. "You know I planned to marry the girl. I still do."

Wray tensed, and Travis said in a low voice, "Not now, Joel. Penny's liable to get hurt." The marshal knew how close his newfound friend was to charging at McCabe, regardless of the consequences.

Wray took a deep breath. "All right," he murmured. "I'll wait to settle the score with you, McCabe."

The rancher laughed again. "You'll wait, all right. Until nine o'clock . . ."

Inside the small cellblock in the sheriff's office, Will Dehner was saying solemnly, "I'm sorry, Ruth. It's time."

A block away from the sheriff's office on the courthouse square, several hundred people milled around, waiting impatiently. The surrounding streets were clogged with horses and wagons, and the sunlit morning air rang with talk and excited laughter. Children ran among the adults, their games and horseplay taking them underfoot and prompting parents to snap at them irritably. If a band had been playing, the gathering could have been mistaken for a Fourth of July celebration.

Standing on the platform in front of the gallows was Phineas Kingsley Nelson. The immaculately groomed hangman was dressed in his best suit, his hat brushed and his boots polished. But his normally cheerful expression was missing, and his face was frozen in grim lines. He had never felt less like cracking a joke in his life. It was five minutes before nine o'clock.

Nelson had awakened long before dawn and tossed restlessly until the sky began to grow bright. In the gray half-light, he dressed and left his hotel without eating breakfast. He combed the town—checking at the Barnes Hotel, stopping at the livery stable where Travis had rented his horse—to see if Luke Travis had returned. He found no sign of the marshal. No one had seen the man from Abilene since he left Cheyenne two days earlier.

Even then, with several hours to spare, Nelson had sensed that Travis was going to be too late to intervene. There would be no last-minute miracle. At nine o'clock Sheriff Dehner would lead Ruth Carson to the gallows to meet her fate. Those last few hours raced by. Nelson had never known time to pass so quickly. The appointed hour was upon them.

As he waited he rested his hand on the new lever and thought about all the work he had done on the mechanism the day before. He replaced all the broken parts and tested it carefully to make sure everything was as it should be. Now, feeling the smooth lever in his hand, the hangman was as certain as he had ever been in his long career that the gallows would do exactly what he wanted it to do.

The crowd began to babble excitedly, and Nelson knew that Ruth and Dehner had emerged from the jail. Peering over the heads of the spectators, he spotted them walking slowly toward the square, the crowd parting before them.

In the lead was the young deputy, Jeremy. His face was pale, and he was carrying a shotgun. Dehner walked right behind him, beside Ruth. The sheriff had one hand on Ruth's arm. She was clad in a simple but elegant dress, and Nelson saw with a pang that she was carrying a small bunch of flowers. Her hands were not tied or cuffed. Her head was high, her features calm and composed. She had never looked lovelier, he thought. He wished he could have gone to the jail earlier and spoken to her one more time.

Two deputies, armed with shotguns, brought up the rear of the little procession. They made sure that the crowd did not press in too closely around the sheriff and the prisoner.

Nelson stared at the approaching group, unable to take his eyes off Ruth. He saw that as people were struck by Ruth's dignity they stopped speaking, and the hubbub began to subside. *Finally,* Nelson thought, *the crowd realizes just how serious this is.*

Jeremy reached the bottom of the stairs, turned, and took up his position on the left side. Ruth and Dehner moved past the deputy and ascended the steps slowly but surely. As Ruth climbed to the gallows, Nelson could see her eyes, could read the fear she was concealing from the crowd. He felt his chest tighten.

Dehner led Ruth across the platform to him. The sheriff took a deep breath and said, "Mr. Nelson, I am hereby turning this prisoner over to you so that you can carry out the sentence imposed by the court."

Nelson nodded gravely and said, "Thank you, Sheriff. Now, if you will kindly step back . . ."

Nodding abruptly, Dehner released Ruth's arm. He turned, strode to the stairs, and walked briskly down them.

Ruth and Nelson were alone on the platform. That was how it usually was, Nelson thought, although sometimes the local authorities stood closer in case of trouble. No one expected Ruth would cause any problems, though. With the huge crowd gathered around the gallows, she had no place to go if she tried to escape.

Nelson murmured, "Hello, Ruth."

"Good morning, Phineas," she replied, her voice surprisingly strong. "It's going to be quite a lovely day, isn't it?"

He glanced at the deep blue sky and said, "Yes, I believe it is."

"I don't blame you for any of this, you know."

Nelson nodded. "I know."

"Have you seen Luke? I thought he would be here."

"I'm afraid no one has seen him, Ruth. He may have run into trouble, wherever he was headed."

"I hope he's all right. He's a good man. We didn't always get along, but I knew my sister wouldn't have married him if he wasn't a good man."

"I'm sure he did everything he could," Nelson replied. He reached into his pocket and took out a folded black hood.

The sight of it provoked a reaction from the crowd. As the muttering grew, Nelson slipped it over Ruth's head while he spoke soothingly to her. Then he caught the dangling noose and slid the loop quickly over her head. Nelson tightened it with practiced ease.

That grim chore done, Nelson went to the head of the stairs and looked down at Dehner. The sheriff was gazing at a pocket watch he held in his hand. Dehner glanced at Nelson and nodded gravely.

Nelson went back to Ruth. He put his hands on her shoulders and shifted her position a few inches on the trapdoor. Then, his face showing no emotion, he walked to the lever at the edge of the platform.

No sound came from the crowd.

The hangman gave the lever a sharp tug. It slid over smoothly, clicking into place. Nelson kept his eyes on the lever, not looking at Ruth and the trapdoor.

Someone in the crowd gasped, and then the spectators burst into a roar of cheering and outrage.

Slowly, Nelson lifted his head and looked toward Ruth. She was still standing on the platform with her back straight and her head held high. The trapdoor had not budged.

Beyond her Sheriff Dehner appeared at the top of the stairs, a surprised and anxious expression on his face. As he came across the platform, he asked urgently, "What happened?"

Nelson shook his head. "The trapdoor didn't work," he said simply.

"Well, try it again, man!" Dehner snapped.

Nelson complied. He pushed the lever back into its original position, then pulled it sharply toward him. Once, twice, three times he repeated the action, and at each attempt the results were the same. The trapdoor stayed firmly in place.

"I don't understand it," Nelson said, shaking his head. The noise of the crowd thundered around the gallows so that the hangman had to shout to make himself heard. "I worked on the mechanism all day yesterday. Everything was perfect."

In the crowd people were yelling and jeering, upset that they would apparently miss the spectacle they had traveled all the way to Cheyenne to see. Glancing nervously at the angry mob, Dehner turned to the hangman and growled, "Goddammit! You'd better do something about this, Nelson."

"I can repair the problem, but it'll take time," Nelson replied grimly. "You'd better get your prisoner back to the jail before some of these folks decide to have their own lynch party."

Dehner nodded. "You're right." He turned to his deputies and called, "Jeremy! You and the others get up here!"

Nelson strode over to Ruth and pulled the black hood off her head. She met his gaze squarely, a tiny smile tugging at the corners of her mouth. "I seem to have cheated the hangman," she said dryly.

"For now," Nelson grunted. He loosened the noose and lifted it over her head.

Dehner caught his arm. "When can you have this thing fixed?" he demanded over the hubbub of the crowd.

"Probably in a couple of hours, but to be certain you'd better allow a little more time than that."

Dehner nodded and turned to face the spectators. "Settle down, you people!" he roared. Then he noticed Jeremy climbing the steps. He reached out and grabbed the young deputy's shotgun. Pointing it toward the sky, Dehner touched off one of the barrels, and the thunderous blast silenced the crowd. The sheriff called out, "The hanging's been rescheduled for twelve o'clock noon! If anybody wants to cause trouble, we can always find another noose!"

No one in the crowd said a word. On the fringes of the throng, people began to drift away, muttering quietly among themselves.

Dehner handed the shotgun back to Jeremy. "Get her back to her cell," he snapped. "And don't let anything happen on the way."

Jeremy nodded. The other deputies and he led Ruth down the steps and back toward the sheriff's office. Dehner cast a long, warning look at Nelson, then followed.

Slowly, the hangman took off his coat and draped it over the railing around the edge of the platform. Then he went down the stairs, ducked underneath the gallows, and got to work.

Luke Travis stood at the window of the room where the prisoners had been taken. McCabe's men had not tied his hands, so he was able to reach into his pocket and take out his watch. He glanced at the sun, then opened the watch and stared at its face. The hands told the story plainly. It was five minutes after nine.

The watch had been given to him by the citizens of Wichita for his years of service as their marshal. That had been several years ago, long before he had come to Abilene. In all those years, the watch had never failed to keep good time.

Travis took a deep breath, snapped the watchcase shut, and slipped it back into his pocket. Closing his eyes, he slowly reached up and rubbed his temples. He felt tears welling behind his eyelids and knew they were for Ruth.

It was too late. Ruth was gone now, as much a victim of someone's evil plot as Mayor Roland T. Yates had been.

Behind Travis, Joel Wray and Penny Yates were sitting on the bed, holding hands and talking quietly. Penny had told Wray and Travis that this was the room where she had been held prisoner the night before. She knew how secure it was and showed them that the window had been nailed shut.

The lovely blonde had regained consciousness a few minutes after they were locked in, and other than a headache, she seemed to be suffering no ill effects from her fall. The first thing she wanted to know was what McCabe intended to do with them.

"He says he's going to marry you," Wray told her.

Penny shuddered. "I'll kill myself first," she declared.

Wray shook his head. "No. That wouldn't solve anything, Penny. Someday, the truth will catch up with McCabe, no matter what happens to us. You've got to stay alive so that you can see that justice is done."

She smiled weakly. "That's quite a burden you're placing on me, Joel."

Wray glanced at Travis's stiff back as the marshal stared out the window. "You may be the only one who can help bring the truth out, Penny," he said softly.

Now, nine o'clock had come and gone, and all they could do was wait.

The time passed with agonizing slowness. McCabe had evidently decided to torture them even more and drag this out. There was nothing for any of them to say. Travis stood at the window, peering out and thinking his own thoughts, while Wray and Penny huddled together and tried to draw what comfort they could from their closeness.

An hour passed before the three of them heard the sound of footsteps approaching in the hall. Travis turned from the window and regarded the two young people sitting on the bed. "I'm sorry I got you into this," he said. "I was just trying to help Ruth."

Wray shook his head. "It's all McCabe's doing, not yours, Luke."

"I don't intend to just give in and let McCabe do whatever he wants," Travis said. "As soon as Penny is in the clear, I'm going to try to jump one of them."

Wray nodded, a muscle twitching slightly in his jaw. "Damn right. I'm with you, Luke."

Penny clutched at his arm. "But Joel, if you cause trouble, they'll kill—" She stopped abruptly, realizing that was exactly what McCabe was planning to do.

"It's all right, darling," Wray said, squeezing her hand.

The key rattled in the lock, and the door swung open. Flint McCabe stood framed in the doorway with a shotgun in his hands. "Downright touching." He sneered as he took in the scene. "I figured you and Penny might have made better use of that bed than just sitting on it, Wray. Wouldn't have bothered me. I don't mind getting used goods."

"You bastard," Wray growled as he came to his feet.

McCabe leveled the shotgun at him. Behind the rancher, several armed cowhands trained their weapons on them. "Just come out of there real slow," McCabe ordered.

Wray put a hand on Penny's shoulder. "You stay here," he said. "No need for you to see this."

McCabe shook his head. "No, I want the girl to

come, too. You won't be leaving my side after this, Penny. You might as well get used to it."

Surrounded by armed men, Travis and Wray could do nothing. McCabe took Penny's arm and held it while the other men prodded Travis and Wray down the stairs, through the door, and onto the veranda.

There were several horses tied to the rack in front of the house. McCabe said, "All right, get them mounted up and take them to Horsehead Meadow. That's the most isolated part of the ranch. Nobody's going to find a couple of fresh graves there."

"Sure, boss." One of the hands nodded.

Before anyone could step off the porch, the sound of a galloping horse made everyone pause. McCabe snapped, "Hold it!" as a rider raced his animal up the trail and sped into the clearing in front of the house. The man was a Trident hand, and he had just about ridden his horse into the ground. The exhausted animal glistened with sweat and stood with its sides heaving while the man dropped from the saddle.

"What the hell is it, Dundee?" McCabe asked.

"I just . . . just got in from town, boss," the rider replied, gasping for breath. "The hangin's been put off!"

"What!" McCabe roared, anger twisting his face.

Travis felt an incredible surge of relief. Somehow, a miracle had taken place.

"The gallows didn't work," the cowboy called Dundee panted. "Don't know what happened, but the sheriff was mad as hell at that hangman feller. They're goin' to try again at twelve o'clock. I flogged it on out here to let you know."

Travis's eyes darted around the porch. Everyone was staring at Dundee, including McCabe. This might be the only chance Wray and he would get. It was a chance Travis was going to take.

"Now!" he yelled to Wray. He lashed out behind him, knocking the gun that had been trained at his back from the cowboy's hands to the porch floor. McCabe started to turn, but he was too late. Travis threw himself at the rancher, slamming into him and forcing him back a couple of steps. The marshal grasped the shotgun McCabe was carrying and wrenched it out of his grip.

Penny cried out in surprise and fear, but her shriek was lost in the roar of the shotgun as Travis whirled around and blasted both barrels at the Trident hands on the veranda. At this close range they never had a chance. The double load of buckshot blew them backward like bloody rag dolls.

At the same moment that Travis had acted, Joel Wray had moved with every bit of speed he could summon, spinning around and driving a hard punch into the face of the man who had been covering him. With his other hand, Wray snatched the pistol out of the guard's hand and started firing at the men who had not been cut down by the shotgun blast.

McCabe launched himself at Travis with a furious yell. Travis spun to meet the charge, whirling the now-empty shotgun as if it were a club. The stock caught McCabe in the chest, knocking the breath out of him and stunning him. Travis slashed at him with the barrels of the weapon. A glancing blow clipped McCabe's head, but it was hard enough to knock him off his feet.

The gunfire drove the horses tied to the hitch rail into a frenzy. Several of them had jerked their reins loose and were skittering away. Wray grabbed Penny's arm and leapt off the porch, heading for the remaining mounts. Penny looked stunned by the violence that had broken out around her, but as Wray all but threw her into the saddle on one of the horses, she gathered her wits and grasped the animal's reins.

He vaulted onto the back of another animal, throwing shots at McCabe's men as he did to give Travis some cover. Travis bounded off the porch and onto a saddle. He yanked the horse's reins free and shouted, "Come on!"

A hail of bullets followed them as they pounded away from the ranch house. McCabe struggled back onto his feet and screamed, "Kill them! Kill all three of them!"

It became obvious a moment later, though, that none of the bullets would reach their targets. Travis, Wray, and Penny were crouching against the necks of their mounts, riding desperately for their lives.

Travis glanced over at Penny Yates. She was handling herself well, staying in the saddle, and getting every ounce of speed from her horse that she could. Wray was right beside her, twisting in the saddle and firing his pistol at the men on the ranch house porch.

McCabe and his men would be coming after them, Travis knew, but they had a few minutes' head start. They had a chance again . . .a chance to make it to Cheyenne by noon.

Chapter Seventeen

———◆———

Several times during that first hour one of Sheriff Dehner's deputies came by the gallows and asked P. K. Nelson if he needed any help with the repairs. Each time, the hangman shook his head. "Coming along just fine," he told the man. Nelson was sure Dehner had sent the deputy to check on the progress of the work.

A little after ten o'clock, Nelson emerged from under the gallows. He noticed many people still hanging around the square, although the crowd was not as large as it had been earlier. The spectators would start drifting back between eleven and twelve.

In the meantime, Nelson had an important chore to do. He retrieved his coat from the platform, then walked down the street to the sheriff's office.

The door was locked. Nelson had to knock and identify himself before Dehner would let him in. As the sheriff swung the door open, he asked anxiously, "Have you got that gallows fixed yet, Nelson?"

"Not yet," Nelson replied. "I've got to go over to the hardware store and pick up a few items to complete the repairs. Some new hinges for one thing. The ones that were on it jammed. They're frozen now, and I don't have time to soak them and break them loose again."

"Well, why are you wasting time here? Go get what you need."

Nelson grinned. "I just wanted you to know where I was, in case that watchdog of yours goes by the gallows again and sees I'm not there."

Dehner grunted but did not deny that he had sent the deputy. He said, "You're taking this mighty calm, Nelson. You know a failure like this is going to hurt your reputation."

"Not much I can do about it now," Nelson said with a shrug. He glanced toward the cellblock door and wished he had time to say hello to Ruth. He decided it would not look very good right now, and besides, he had less than two hours to find what he was looking for.

"Do you still think everything will be ready by noon?"

"It will," Nelson assured the sheriff. With a nod, he left the office, pausing on the sidewalk outside as he heard Dehner relock the door.

Ruth would be safe enough until noon, Nelson thought. The crowd had threatened to turn ugly for a moment after the gallows had failed, but that had been a temporary reaction. Mayor Yates had not had enough friends to provoke a lynching.

Ruth's biggest danger now was that Nelson would

not be able to take advantage of this last-minute opportunity to prove her innocence.

The key was in those papers that Simon Smith had returned to Penny Yates. Nelson was convinced of that. Although Malcolm Ebersole had tried to disguise his own interest in them, Nelson knew that the young newspaperman thought they were important, too.

Nelson had hesitated to involve Penny in this, but now there was no time to do anything else. Instead of going to the hardware store as he had told Dehner, Nelson went directly to the Yates house. He was going to ask Penny to show him those papers, and he would not take no for an answer.

By themselves the documents probably would not clear Ruth of the murder, but they were now evidence and would cast doubt on her guilt and suggest that someone else had a motive. Judge Shaw and Sheriff Dehner had said all along they regretted the outcome of the trial. Now Nelson planned to persuade them to reconsider and postpone the execution until all of Yates's business dealings could be brought out into the open.

Nelson had not seen Penny Yates at the hanging, but that meant nothing. She could well have been there among the large crowd. He just hoped that she was at home now.

He reached the late mayor's house and went up the walk to the front porch. The curtains were drawn, and the place looked quiet. Not unusual under the circumstances, Nelson thought. Penny was probably upstairs lying down. He climbed the steps to the porch and started to knock on the front door.

Nelson stopped before he could rap on the panel, a frown forming on his round face. The door was slightly ajar, no more than an inch or so but definitely open. That struck him as strange. He put a hand against the door and slowly pushed it.

The foyer was shadowy. Nelson stepped inside and paused again. He thought he had heard a slight sound coming from his right, from the parlor. Some instinct was warning him that he was heading into trouble. He slipped a hand into his coat and closed his fingers around the butt of his S&W .38, the little Baby Russian.

A dim figure suddenly moved in the gloom of the parlor, and Nelson jerked the pistol out. Leveling it at the figure, he growled, "Hold it, mister!"

The shape froze, and a moment later a familiar voice asked, "Is that you, Mr. Nelson?"

The hangman frowned. "Ebersole? What are you doing here?" Before the newspaperman could answer, Nelson stepped over to the window and thrust back the curtain.

The bright sunlight from outside revealed Malcolm Ebersole standing next to the chimney. The sleeve of his light gray jacket was covered with black smudges that Nelson recognized as soot. Clutched tightly in Ebersole's hand was a thick sheaf of papers.

A light brighter than that streaming in through the window seemed to go off in P. K. Nelson's brain.

"I'm certainly glad to see you, Mr. Nelson," Ebersole began excitedly. "Something seems to have happened to Miss Yates. The house was all closed up when I got here—"

"When you came looking for those papers, you mean," Nelson cut in. His mind was spinning rapidly, checking and rechecking each facet of the theory that had just occurred to him. There were still some unanswered questions, but what he knew so far made sense. He had no idea where Penny Yates was, but he would have been willing to bet she was in danger.

"These papers?" Ebersole said, holding them up and trying to sound baffled.

Something lying on the sofa caught Nelson's eye. It was a dress, he saw, a dress with soot smudges on the sleeve. That had been enough of a clue to send Ebersole in here to the fireplace. Nelson nodded to himself. Penny had some sort of hiding place inside the chimney, and that was where she had concealed the papers. Why she had hidden them, Nelson did not know, but he had a hunch a quick look at them would provide the answer.

"Hand them over," he said.

Ebersole hesitated, swallowing nervously. The barrel of the .38 in Nelson's hand never wavered. The hangman had long since lost his jovial demeanor. Now he looked positively deadly.

Ebersole held out the papers. Nelson took them, backed up a couple of steps, and took his eyes off the younger man just long enough to glance at what was written on the documents. They appeared to be some sort of business records, no doubt pertaining to the activities of Mayor Roland Yates and Flint McCabe.

"I guess you thought you were reclaiming something that belonged to you," Nelson grunted, "since you probably stole these from Yates in the first place."

"I never stole anything!" Ebersole replied hotly.

"Yates wouldn't have given these to you. I'd wager they have to do with some illegal activities that the late mayor and his partner were engaged in. You got your hands on them, hid them in the newspaper office, and used them to blackmail Yates and McCabe, didn't you?"

Ebersole gaped at him for a long moment. Then he said abruptly, "I don't have to talk to you. I'm going to swear out a complaint against you, Nelson. You can't come in here, wave a gun, and make these crazy accusations—"

"Fine," Nelson broke in. "We'll go see Sheriff Dehner right now. You can explain to him what you were doing in this house with these documents."

Ebersole took a step forward, his face contorting angrily. "They're mine!" he rasped. "You're trying to ruin everything—"

"Just stand still," Nelson said coldly, lining up the barrel of the .38 with the bridge of Ebersole's nose. "You're going to listen to me, and then you're going to tell me if I'm right about all this." He took a deep breath. "It's simple enough, once you look at it from the proper angle. Yates and McCabe were well on their way to running this whole territory, but you had proof that not only had they gotten a crooked start in their business, they were still breaking the law." Nelson hefted the stack of papers for emphasis. "You probably didn't blackmail them for money, not yet. Ruth told me you were ambitious. You wanted power, Ebersole. You wanted to be the third leg of that trident they use for a brand."

"You son of a bitch," Ebersole hisséd, and Nelson knew his speculations were right on target.

"Being a newspaperman, you figured that, if you had your own paper, you would have the perfect vehicle for the power you intended to get through Yates and McCabe. And what was the easiest way for you to get your hands on a newspaper? *You planned to take Ruth Carson's!"*

Ebersole clenched his fists, his whole body quivering with rage. "You don't know what it was like!" he shot back. "You damned hypocrite! You made your reputation hanging people! I just wanted what was due me . . . !"

Nelson shook his head. "Ruth would have retired someday. In all probability the paper would have been yours then. But you couldn't wait. You decided that she had to go now." Nelson felt his heart pounding, and his mouth was dry. He ached to pull the trigger of the little gun. "You tried to kill her, didn't you, Ebersole? She said you were there at her house when Yates came to dinner. You slipped the poison in something then. But Yates got hold of it instead of Ruth! You killed him by accident, didn't you?" Nelson's voice had risen until he was shouting the question.

For a moment, he thought Ebersole was going to lunge at him. Nelson was ready to shoot. But he wanted to take the young man alive, if possible, so that Ebersole would be forced to tell the truth and clear Ruth Carson.

Then Ebersole seemed to get control of himself. He smiled thinly and said, "It all worked out for the best. Ruth was going to be hanged, the paper was mine to run, and Yates was dead. That meant more money for McCabe and me to split."

"McCabe knew all about it, didn't he?"

"Of course he did. I had to tell him when Yates died instead of Ruth. He didn't give a damn about Yates. In fact, he seemed pleasantly surprised."

Nelson nodded. "So you thought everything had

worked out just right for you. The only problem was that Simon Smith got overzealous in his cleaning and returned these papers to Penny Yates. You figured you had to get them back, and you thought this morning would be a good time to search the house, while everyone else in town was all wrapped up with the hanging." Nelson frowned as another thought occurred to him. "You know where Penny Yates is, don't you?"

"McCabe has her. I got word from him last night. She's not going to cause any trouble for us, Nelson, and neither are you. You can't prove one damn word of this insane yarn of yours." Ebersole grinned smugly. "I'm a respected citizen in this town, and so is McCabe. You're going to have to go out there and hang Ruth, just like the court sentenced her."

Nelson shook his head. "I don't think so. These documents will be enough to create a reasonable doubt, maybe even get Ruth a new trial. You had as much access to that poison at the newspaper office as Ruth did, and you've got a motive."

"Like I said, you can't prove a thing about motive or anything else."

"We'll see," Nelson said grimly. He gestured with the pistol. "Come on. We're going to see Sheriff Dehner."

Ebersole shook his head stubbornly. "I'm not going anywhere," he declared.

Nelson tightened his grip on the pistol. If need be, he was willing to shoot Ebersole in the leg and drag him to Dehner's office.

A sudden flurry of gunfire blasting outside made him jerk his head toward the window. The shots sounded as though they were coming from the edge of town, and they were rapidly getting closer.

Nelson instantly realized he had made a mistake by turning his attention away from Ebersole. The murderous newspaperman had taken advantage of the opportunity and was leaping at him.

As the hangman tried to whirl around, Ebersole grabbed his wrist and forced the gun to the side with desperate strength. At the same time, he brought his knee up, driving it savagely into Nelson's groin. Nelson tried to wrench the gun back in line as he gasped in pain, but Ebersole was savagely fighting like a madman.

Nelson staggered back as Ebersole smashed an elbow against his jaw. He felt the pistol being torn out of his grip. Suddenly the gun went off, and what felt like a white-hot poker rammed into Nelson's body. He grunted, doubling over from the pain. He tried to catch himself as he fell, but it was too late.

Nelson pitched forward onto the floor of the parlor. The room seemed shadowy as he struggled to pull himself to his feet, despite the bright sunshine slanting in through the window. He blinked his eyes as he saw Malcolm Ebersole drop the gun, then bend over and scoop the fallen documents from the floor. Ebersole seemed to be moving incredibly slowly. It would not be hard at all, Nelson thought, to reach out and stop him. He tried to lift a hand to do that, but before he could, the shadows closed in.

Nelson's head fell to the side, and his hand dropped to the floor. He sprawled there, motionless except for that hand. The fingers stretched out, tried to clutch at something for a moment, then went limp.

The front door slammed behind Ebersole as the newspaperman ran out, but Nelson could no longer hear it.

If it had not been for Joel Wray's knowledge of the terrain, Travis knew they never would have had a chance of reaching Cheyenne in time. But the young cowboy had taken the lead and found every shortcut, every path where the three desperate riders could put a little distance between themselves and their pursuers. Their horses were fresh, and the animals performed gallantly.

But McCabe's men had fresh mounts, too, and every time Travis and the others managed to open up a small gap, the Trident riders closed it in a matter of minutes.

Travis glanced over his shoulder and saw McCabe riding in the lead, perhaps a hundred yards behind them. They were within rifle range, but it was almost impossible to hit a moving target from the back of a running horse. A few of the shots fired by McCabe and his men had come close enough for Travis to hear them whining past his ear, but so far Wray, Penny, and he were unscathed.

The cowboy named Dundee had made the trip from Cheyenne to Trident in a little over an hour. This deadly chase was going to take about the same amount of time, Travis estimated.

It was one of the longest hours of his life. But knowing that Ruth's life had been spared temporarily made him that much more determined to get through.

Finally Wray called out, "Cheyenne!" Travis could see the buildings ahead and knew that they would reach the town in a matter of minutes. He glanced over at Penny. She was hanging on grimly, but he could tell that fear and the long chase had exhausted her. He hoped she could hold on for just a little while longer.

Behind them, McCabe and his men had flogged their horses and closed the gap to about fifty yards. Their shots were coming nearer. If McCabe could kill the three of them now, he could still get away with it.

Travis leaned over the neck of his horse and urged it to draw on its last reserves of speed and strength.

Suddenly he realized their mounts were running on the main road into town rather than on the trail to Trident. Buildings flashed by, and Travis glimpsed the startled faces of the townspeople who watched them gallop past. Wray was still in the lead, and he was headed for the sheriff's office. McCabe's men had no choice but to stop firing. They could not gun the three of them down in front of witnesses.

Wray hauled his horse to a stop in front of Dehner's office. Travis was right behind him. The young cowhand snagged the reins of Penny's mount and dragged it to a halt. Drawn by the commotion, Dehner burst out of his office. His deputies were right behind him, and all of them carried guns.

Travis slid from the saddle and glanced up the street. McCabe and his men had slowed their horses to a trot now, but they were still coming. The rancher's face was set in murderous lines.

Wray helped Penny down from her horse and clutched her to him. She was sobbing hysterically, giving in to the strain she had been under for so long. Dehner looked at her, then at Travis. "What the bloody hell's going on here?" he demanded.

"You tell him, Penny," Travis suggested grimly.

"He kidnapped me!" Penny wailed, huddling in Wray's arms.

"Kidnapped? By God, girl, who kidnapped you?" Dehner asked.

"Flint McCabe!" The name was torn out of Penny.

"That's a goddamned lie," McCabe said icily. He sat on his horse a few feet away, his men behind him. Leveling an accusing finger at Travis and Wray, he went on. "Those two just robbed my ranch, and they took Miss Penny as a hostage! All of my men will tell you that's the truth, Sheriff."

Dehner looked back and forth between the accusing parties, clearly confused. "But she says you kidnapped her, McCabe," he said.

"She's overwrought because of her father's death," McCabe said smoothly. "She's imagining things because she's so upset, Sheriff. You can understand that."

Travis met McCabe's eyes and saw a trace of mockery there. The rancher was smooth, all right. Travis had to give him that much. He must have come up with this story on the way into town while he was doing his best to kill them. Travis looked back at Dehner and saw that the sheriff was rubbing his jaw in puzzlement. McCabe was an influential man in this part of the country. His story was pretty weak, but Dehner appeared to be wavering. The sheriff was on the verge of accepting what McCabe had to say.

A crowd had gathered in front of the sheriff's office, its numbers swelled by the people who had come to Cheyenne to witness the hanging.

Travis scanned the group, hoping to see someone who might help, who might speak up and force Dehner to listen to reason. Suddenly he spotted

Malcolm Ebersole on the boardwalk a few feet away. Travis was about to call his name when he noticed Ebersole's disheveled condition. More important, he caught the glance that the young newspaperman exchanged with Flint McCabe. Ebersole patted his jacket pocket, as if to assure McCabe that he had something safely stored there. The gesture was surreptitious, and Travis doubted that anyone in the crowd noticed it except him.

Ebersole and McCabe? Suddenly a great many things started to make sense to Luke Travis. The only problem was, it looked as if it was too late to do anything about them.

Dehner stepped forward and clamped a hand on Travis's arm. "You and Wray had better come with me, Travis," he growled. "We'll get to the bottom of this."

"No!" one of McCabe's men suddenly yelled. "They're robbers and kidnappers! String 'em up!"

The spectators on the boardwalk took up the cry. Shouts of "Hang 'em!" resounded through the street. The crowd had been cheated of one hanging today. They did not intend to miss out on another one.

McCabe was grinning now. Everything was going his way. Dehner and his deputies were pale and nervous, and it was clear to Travis that they might not be willing to stop a lynch mob, even if they had been able. The man from Kansas looked again at Ebersole, saw the smile on his face.

"Ebersole!" called a voice.

The newspaperman stiffened and turned as several people on the boardwalk near him suddenly backed away. As he saw who had called his name Ebersole cried, "Oh, my God . . ."

P. K. Nelson was lurching along the boardwalk toward him. A huge bloodstain spread across the hangman's shirt and coat, but his eyes were clear and determined as he closed in on Ebersole. His .38 was in his hand.

In a frighteningly cold voice Nelson said, "You should have made sure I was dead, Ebersole. I want those papers."

Ebersole was panting harshly as he stared at Nelson. Suddenly he seemed to break out of the trance that was gripping him. He lunged toward one of the bystanders and jerked the man's pistol from its holster. Uttering an inarticulate cry, Ebersole spun toward Nelson and lifted the gun.

The hangman fired. The bullet struck Ebersole in the shoulder, knocking him backward. The gun he had grabbed fell from his hand, unfired.

Dehner yelled, "What the devil!" The people in the street scattered, looking for cover in case there was more shooting.

Travis saw Flint McCabe's hand darting toward his holstered gun. McCabe had to know the game was over, that he was about to be exposed as a rustler and maybe a killer and God knew what else. But a man like McCabe would not want to go down alone.

With one hand Travis suddenly shoved Sheriff Dehner to the side while he snatched the rifle from his grip with the other. McCabe was lifting his gun when Travis fired from the hip, the rifle blasting in his hands. One shot erupted from McCabe's gun, but the bullet went high in the air as the rancher threw his hands up and plunged from the saddle. He landed heavily in the dusty street, dead from the Winchester slug that had slammed into his chest an instant earlier.

Travis heard the clicking of hammers being cocked and looked around to see Dehner's deputies pointing their guns at him. He stood very still, not wanting anyone's trigger finger to get itchy. McCabe's men sat unmoving on their horses, clearly confused as to what to do now that their boss was dead. Wray still had his arms around Penny. No one moved until Nelson limped forward and bent over Ebersole, who was squirming and whimpering from the pain of his wounded shoulder. Nelson reached inside Ebersole's coat and pulled out a sheaf of papers. He walked slowly over to Sheriff Dehner and thrust the documents at him.

"You'd better read these, Sheriff," he said. "And then you'd better have a long talk with Ebersole as soon as he's patched up. I imagine Luke Travis and his young friend have some pretty important things to tell you, too."

Dehner opened and closed his mouth several times, then finally managed to stammer, "B-but what about the hanging?"

Nelson shook his head. "There's not going to be any hanging. Not today. And if you'll excuse me, there's someone inside that jail I want to break that news to personally."

With a broad grin on his face, Nelson clapped Travis on the shoulder and then turned toward the office. Despite the blood from his wound, Nelson looked like his old self again, Travis thought, like that jolly fellow he had met on the train from Abilene.

Right now, P. K. Nelson was just about the happiest hangman Luke Travis had ever seen.

Chapter Eighteen

———◆———

QUITE A CROWD HAD GATHERED AT CHEYENNE'S TRAIN station to see Luke Travis off the next morning. P. K. Nelson and Ruth Carson were there, along with Penny Yates and Joel Wray. They were a pair of fine-looking couples, Travis thought. Sheriff Will Dehner was on hand, too, as was the young deputy, Jeremy. At one end of the platform, Simon Smith leaned on the railing and used it to support the pad on which he was sketching the big Baldwin locomotive.

It had taken the remainder of the previous day to sort everything out, but once Dehner had learned what had happened both in Cheyenne and at the Trident ranch, he was convinced of Ruth's innocence. Together with Judge Franklin Shaw, Dehner visited Malcolm Ebersole at the local doctor's office, and the wounded newspaperman quickly broke down and confessed to his part in the murder of Mayor Yates.

Armed with that testimony and the records Nelson had recovered, Judge Shaw convened his court just long enough to dismiss all charges against Ruth Carson.

Now, as she took Travis's hand while they stood on the depot platform, Ruth asked, "Are you sure you won't stay longer, Luke? With everything that was going on, we hardly got to visit."

Travis smiled and shook his head. "I think I'd better get back to Abilene. I'm sure everything is all right there"—he shrugged his shoulders—"but you know how old lawmen are. We worry about our towns."

"I certainly worried about mine for a while there yesterday," Dehner grunted. He extended a hand to Travis. "Sorry we didn't get to work together more, Marshal. I appreciate what you did. It would have been a terrible mistake if we had . . . well . . ."

Ruth laughed. "I think we know what you're trying to say, Sheriff."

A grin tugged at Dehner's mouth. He snorted, nodded curtly, said, "So long, Travis," and left the platform, with Jeremy following behind him.

Travis looked at Nelson. The hangman probably should have been in bed, he knew, recuperating from the bullet wound Ebersole had given him. The slug had passed through his body, missing the vital organs but knocking Nelson out for a few minutes from shock and loss of blood. But he had come to in time to save Travis, Wray, and Penny, not to mention Ruth.

"I guess you'll be staying here in Cheyenne for a while," Travis said. "You'll need to rest up."

"Indeed he will," Ruth replied, slipping her arm through Nelson's. "Phineas is going to help me with the paper as soon as he feels up to it."

Travis grinned. "Phineas?"

Nelson frowned and shook his head. "Let's not mention that again, shall we? But yes, I plan on staying around for a while. I'm thinking about giving up my career as a hangman." He leaned closer to Travis. "I almost have to, you know."

"Reckon so," Travis said with a chuckle. "Who's going to hire a hangman who rigs his own gallows so it won't work?"

Nelson glanced sharply at Ruth, then looked back at Travis. "Now, how in the world did you know that?"

"I didn't tell him," Ruth said. "I didn't even know about it until you told me just before the hanging."

Travis said, "Don't worry, Nelson. None of us is going to say anything. As for how I knew . . . Well, let's just say I figured a man like you knew his business too well for something like that to be an accident."

Nelson grinned sheepishly. "That's the first time I've ever done anything like that. But I just couldn't hang Ruth. When I broke the mechanism accidentally the day before, I got the idea to repair it so that it would never work again. I'm sure glad I didn't have to go through with the execution."

"So am I," Ruth said. Her smile faded as she went on. "But I am sorry that it turned out to be Malcolm who was responsible for everything. I genuinely liked him. I thought he had the makings of a fine newspaperman." She brightened again. "But the *Eagle* will carry on."

"Of course it will," Travis assured her. He turned to Wray and Penny and thrust out his hand. "Thanks for everything, Joel. None of us would have come through this without your help."

"Glad to do it," Wray replied, shaking Travis's hand firmly. "We'll miss you around here, Luke. Things have sure been popping since you came to town."

"You'll be staying busy enough." Travis grinned as Penny blushed at his words. "You're going to help Miss Penny here take care of that ranch, aren't you?"

"It's all hers, now that McCabe's dead," Wray said. "The way all of his riders ran off yesterday, we're going to have to find a whole new crew. It'll take a lot of work"—his arm tightened around Penny's shoulders—"but I reckon it'll be worth it."

The train conductor came along the platform then, bawling out his summons for the passengers to board. Travis shook hands with Nelson, then kissed Ruth on the cheek. "We'll get together again," he promised, "only under better circumstances."

"I'm going to hold you to that, Luke," she said warmly.

Travis climbed onto the rear platform, waving as the train pulled out of the station. He stayed there until the depot shrank from sight, then went inside the car to find a seat for the long ride home.

He hoped things had been quieter in Abilene than they had been in Wyoming Territory.

Deputy Cody Fisher was waiting at the station when the train carrying Marshal Luke Travis pulled into Abilene a day and a half later. He greeted Travis with a broad grin and said, "Hello, Marshal. Glad to have you back. We were sure happy to get that wire from you about your sister-in-law being innocent and all."

Travis warmly shook hands with his young deputy

and said earnestly, "I'm glad to be back, Cody." He turned toward the baggage car to reclaim his bag. "How was everything while I was gone? Any trouble?"

Cody shrugged. "Oh, nothing to speak of. Nestor Gilworth broke out of jail, but I got him back. He said he was sorry he did it and promised not to do it again."

Travis stopped and turned to stare at Cody. "Broke out?" he exclaimed. "How the devil did he manage to do that?"

"Now, I'm still not sure about that," Cody said with a shake of his head. "You see, I was off fighting that prairie fire with Orion when it happened."

"Prairie fire," Travis said slowly.

"Don't worry, it didn't amount to much. We stopped it before it got to town. Closest it got was burning up a couple of pens out at the Great Western's stockyard. And you'd never even notice that, what with the damage from the stampede and all."

"Stampede?"

"Well, the fire spooked the cattle, of course," Cody said reasonably. "So you can see why I'm not sure just how Nestor managed to get out of his cell. If I hadn't gone looking for him, though, I wouldn't have run into those boys who robbed the bank down in Wichita—"

Travis held up a hand, palm out in surrender. "Never mind," he said. "You can tell me all about it later."

"Sure, Marshal." Cody grinned. "So, how was Wyoming Territory?"